ELEPHANTINA

An Account of
The Accidental Death
of an Elephant

in Dundee in the year 1706, described by
an Engraver resident in that Town.

———

Together with
some *Short Remarks* on
the *Hall of Rarities*,
and the *Life of*
Dr. Patrick Blair,
including *Extracts* from
his remarkable *Essay*

OSTEOGRAPHIA
ELEPHANTINA
TAODUNENSIS

published by
The Royal Society
of London in 1710,

———

THE WHOLE
PRESENTED TO THE PUBLIC BY
'SENEX',
DUNDEE, 1830

CONTENTS

A PROLOGUE

BY A 'FRIEND OF HISTORY'

Five years ago, in the cold September of 1825, a season in which a gentleman feels the need to lay in coals and seek out warmer under-clothes, our attention was drawn to a letter in *The Dundee, Perth and Cupar Advertiser* which offered some details of an event in Dundee's history, of which but few of our citizens were aware – *viz*, the death and subsequent dissection of an Elephant upon our very door-step.

Dr. Patrick Blair, our famous son of Dundee, was the learned surgeon who undertook the anatomical examination in 1706, and the writer of the letter referred us not only to Dr. Blair's celebrated Essay: the *Osteographia Elephantina Taodunensis* which was published in London by the Royal Society, in the year 1710; but also to Dr. Blair's 'Hall of Rarities', which housed here in our city the skeleton of the famous Elephant.

This letter stirred up in us some memories from our youth, for we well remember the 'Hall of Rarities' in this town. Sadly, it is no more. But our memories impelled us to write a short piece for the news-paper, which the Editor was kind enough to print. There, one might have conjectured, the story ended. But we are a man who has engaged in deep and exhaustive study of the History of our County for so long that we do not readily abandon the hint of an untold story.

Therefore, we decided that we would look into the true story of the Elephant of Dr. Blair, and the origin and fate of the 'Hall of Rarities'. After surmounting considerable obstacles to investigation, we established from Mr. W. B. of Boston in Lincoln-shire that the year 1828 would be 100 years exactly since Dr. Patrick Blair had been called to his Maker. We made a determination to complete our researches and sign a *Contract* with a printer to publish our findings to co-incide with that commemoration.

In the manner of Mungo Park, Hugh Clapperton, John Ross and John Cochrane, we travelled across much of the known and unknown world in our search. We jour-neyed to Forfar; we visited Coupar Angus; we witnessed the arrival of the post-coach from London, and felt a cold *shiver* at the sight of *far-travelled* mud on the wheels. We even stood briefly upon the *creaking boards* of a ship pre-paring its sails for Holland, contemplating a sea-voyage so fraught with danger that, although we remained out-wardly bold, we were inwardly in great agitation. Where, our Readers might ask, did we not venture to go in pur-suit of *Knowledge* and for the sole purpose that the Truth about Dr. Blair and the Elephant of Dundee might be laid before the world? Where, indeed?

We understand, from certain correspondence shown to us, that Sir Hans Sloane, of the Royal Society in London, and several of his learned colleagues, held Dr. Blair's knowledge and botanical experience in high re-gard. Had Dr. Blair not, after all, been an Apothecary and Surgeon for many years, in Holland, in Scotland, and in England? Had he not made a Botanical or Physic Garden here in Dundee which was the envy of half of Europe; and was the only garden to be 'in the skies', being held up by the arches of Scott's Close? Had he not, in the early years of his profession, prepared for publication a work whose very title should astound, amaze and divert: '*Manuductio ad Anatomiam*, or a Plain and Easy Method of Dissecting, Preparing, or Preserving all the Parts of the Body of Man, either for Public Demonstration or the Satisfaction of Private Curiosity' (which work, alas, remains unpublished)? Had he not given lectures at our great University of St Andrews? Had he not established a 'Natural History Society' here in Dundee? Had he not corresponded with the esteemed botanist M.Tournefort of Paris, whose death was declared by Dr. Patrick Blair to be 'a general loss to the vegetable kingdom'? What else did Dr. Patrick Blair, *Great Son of Dundee* not do, we wonder?

Alas: while my tireless investigations were in progress, our printer – acting in impertinent self-interest – ascertained that no one in Dundee, or indeed in the whole of Scotland and England, had any thought of marking the 100th year since Dr. Blair's death: on hearing which unpromising news, he swiftly adopted the *Recourse of the Meek*, and declared himself no longer contracted to print our book. There can be no thing more dastardly, more calculated to offend a man of principle than: *Cowardice*. When all the world is clamouring for books of geography and history, when Mr. John Murray in London has all the Adventurers of the world walking through his door – Mr. Prometheus Smith of Dundee makes his apologies. So much for the Integrity of Printers.

We were further delayed by another matter: our discovery of a journal written by Mr. Gilbert Orum, resident of Dundee in 1706. After reading an advertisement which

we had placed for any information touching on the matter
under examination, a descendant of Mr. Orum, then living in Dunfermline, wrote to notify us that he possessed
a journal written by his ancestor, whose subject was the
famous Elephant. Our correspondent was persuaded to
pass the papers on to us, rather than using them to light 'a
last pipe' before embarking on a new life across the ocean.
(Why he could not have brought this to our attention earlier, and so saved us considerable trouble, we fail to understand. This gentleman perished in the snow-fields of
Canada in 1829, having been in that untamed country for
precisely eight days. So much for Canada.) Mr. Gilbert
Orum, it appeared from this Journal, was an engraver who
undertook small commissions for Dr. Blair; we soon veri-
fied that they were his engravings which graced the pages
of Dr. Blair's famous Essay on the Elephant, published
by the Royal Society of London.

But let the Reader be warned: Mr. Orum's Journal
is a Libel – do not make the mistake of judging it otherwise. It is not to be relied upon. It is so poorly written, so
manifestly full of Deceit, Calumny, Slander and Scandal,
that we stood several times *anguished* before the fire,
poised to turn the papers to ashes. Only our life-long
Dedication to *Truth* stayed our hand, that almost all of
the Journal might see the light of day, that our Readers
might learn for themselves how History is written and yet
how it should *not* be written: 'By its Darkness, we may see
Light.' Throughout, we have corrected the orthography;
here and there, we have made some discreet remarks and
observations by which we have illuminated the text for
the Reader.

We have found another printer, Mr. Mercurius

McAndrew, who has been persuaded by the promise of great personal profit to print our edition of the 'Journal of Gilbert Orum'. His only stipulation was that we make the book 'not too long': we have acceded to this – let him now fulfil his own obligations.

So much for the Prologue.

'SENEX'
Dundee, July 1830

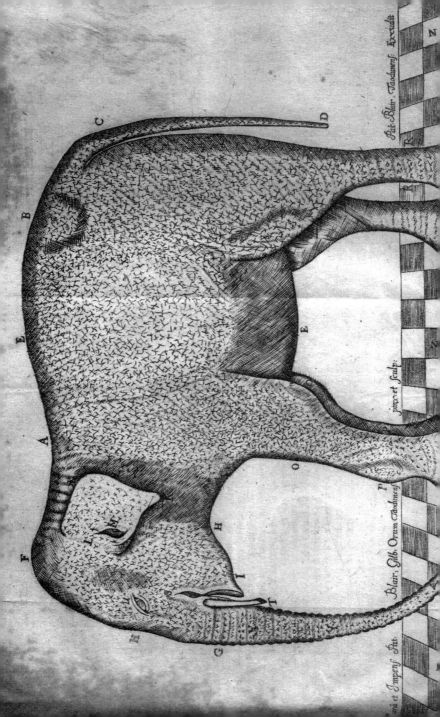

pinxet Sculp:

Blair, Gilb. Orum Taodinenf.

irá et Imperf: Pat.

Tab 2

Cura et Impens: Fr: Blair Gilb: Orim Tadineß pinx et sculp.

Fr: Blair Tadineß

THE JOURNAL
OF GILBERT ORUM

27 APRIL 1706.

At last, all being silent, I am able to embark upon my project, which is to compile a 'Journal'. It is required for the days ahead. Who will read it, I cannot tell, it matters not. I light a small stub of a candle, furnish myself with pen and some paper, draw my chair to the table, place my feet upon Mr. Santos's comfortable thighs, and the paper upon Giovanni's heaving chest. I begin.

———•———

At ten of the morning of Saturday, this seven-and-twentieth day of April 1706, Dr. Blair's man-servant, James Menteith, hammered upon the door to our room, demanding my attendance. Supposing that the surgeon required me, as he has done frequently in the past, to make a graphical record of the performance of some bloody surgical manoeuvre; such as the amputation of a limb, or the extraction of a canker, perhaps the removal of a stone from a man's troubled tripes – manoeuvres which I find utterly abominable, but necessary for the contents of my purse; or that he required me for some small commission, to draw and engrave on copper certain botanical items as he showed an interest in; I pulled on my coat, abandoned my family, and hastened into the morning.

Mr. Menteith refused to impart to me the nature of this urgent business, contenting himself with an uncouth witticism at the expense of Dr. Blair's cook, a lady of some forty years, abandoned by several suitors who preferred a life at sea to a life in her arms; Menteith coarsely suggest-ed by-the-by that my own time to perform ****** upon the cook's **** had arrived;[1] he leered at me, showing his black and yellow teeth. My concern increased by the instant, since Mr. Menteith has a very persuasive tongue. However, on arrival at Dr. Blair's house, I was relieved not to be embraced by the cook; but to be commanded to climb into a carriage with Dr. Blair, for an expedition in the direction of Broughty Ferry; a place in which I knew there to be no ladies;[2] I would not be obliged today to commit the sins of Adultery and Fornication.[3]

Not a mile from Dundee, we came across an excited crowd. I was greatly agitated by this circumstance, imagining a road-side battle, for which – alas – the people of this part of the world are famed, more commonly on a Saturday night. Dr. Blair did not share with me the reason for our presence here. We climbed down and found, having battled through the throng, the corpse of a vast animal.

I had no idea what it was. I have seen pictures of whales, but it was not one of those monsters. It was like a ship-wreck upon the land, broken, cast ashore by departed waves, great heaps of useless canvas covering snapped masts and an abandoned hull. It was like a carriage that

---

1. We have elided here and hereinafter words of a *prurient* nature such as those which Mr. Orum had written here. They are scarcely appropriate for a genteel audience.

2. While we concede that this may be true, only a scoundrel would remark upon it.

3. It is impossible to conceive of any situation in which a man would be *obliged* to commit such a sin against Decency and Marriage. Our Moral Duty was to remove this remark by Mr. Orum – but our Editorial Duty compelled us leave it in the public gaze.

had calamitously fallen from the road, wheels crushed upon the rocks, all movement smashed. My mastery of words is not fit — would that I had had the time to draw it as I first saw it! — I can see it now only as a man fleetingly remembers a dream. It was huge — five or six times the size of a bull, perhaps ten times, it was hard to estimate; its skin grey and scabbed brown like the side of a wild mountain; its head freakish, oppressive, with a face that in death was like no other face I have seen, wise, perhaps — or evil; and a nose — or some powerful cankerous growth that emerged from its broad forehead where its nose should be — that lay upon the ground like a small tree. I could think of no name for it. I could not imagine where it had come from. I held my breath and gazed upon it. My eyes tried to remember every detail. It was not possible. The lines of the body carried me beyond understanding. I could not see how the head joined with the body — the back was too long, the head too vast, there was no neck. Even now, as I write, my breath catches with wonder; I shake my head to clear my thoughts.[4]

It was some time before my eyes came back to me; with difficulty, I forced my gaze away and tried to rec´ognize some of the people gathered there. First and foremost among them, as he had to be, was Mr. George Yeaman,[5] exercising his unquestioned authority as mag´

---

4. Dr. Blair observes, in his famous Essay:

    " 'Tis certainly an Animal of considerable Bigness."

5. Mr. Yeaman was elected as Provost of Dundee in June 1706, a post which he honourably filled until 1708; and again between 1710 and 1712. Between 1710 and 1715, he represented the Perth Burghs at Westminster. All who knew him testified to his great integrity and

istrate, beating back the surrounding on-lookers with his stick; ably assisted in this exercise by three of his servants. Among those whom he fended off from the immediate adjacency of the corpse was a red-faced, tear-stained young man, evidently in the highest transports of grief, who had to be repelled time and time again as he hurled himself forward time and again at the huge beast. Another man, more disciplined, but in foreign hat, argued loudly with Mr. Yeaman; in response to the man's every remark, question, appeal and threat, Mr. Yeaman brandished a sheaf of papers: "You have turned the corpse over to the authorities of this town, sir," he lectured sternly, "and can have no more dealings with it!"

My astonishment was now complete; I could not comprehend how such a huge creature as lay in death before us could be the subject of an ordinary business transaction in which Mr. Yeaman was interested. My wonder was not lessened when Dr. Blair advised his servant Menteith, without troubling himself to include me in the remark, that this dead beast was an 'Elephant'. What was I to think — I had heard of such a beast, but knew not what it looked like. An Elephant, I asked Menteith, here in Dundee? How came it here? What purpose had it in dying here? James Menteith, as might be expected, sneered at me and gave no useful answer: he expected me to believe that Mr. Yeaman had expelled it from his bowels.

Immediately upon Blair's arrival, Mr. Yeaman approached with a smile upon his face. "So, Dr. Blair," says he, "I shall have the pelt and you shall have the meat and

---

his paternal concern for his home-town.

bones, eh?" It was clear from his tone that the two gentlemen had some project in mind, that might not be to the
benefit of the creature.

My patron shook his right hand on the deal, and indicated the massing crowd with his left: "But how are we
to …?" he asked.

The scene before us did, in truth, seem uncommonly
prejudicial to any private business transaction. Six or
seven men were already engaged with large knives, axes,
oars, plough-blades, spades, or whatever they might have
found to hand at the propitious moment, in cutting, hack-
ing and sawing at the flesh of the dead creature; urged on
in their endeavours by a collection of their women-folk,
who saw, for perhaps the first time in the year, a grand
feast lying waiting for them. By way of answer, Mr.
Yeaman showed that thick skin and character of authority
which has always marked him out from the common mass
of humanity; he threatened the crowd with summary execution, eviction and loss of livelihood if they continued to
carry away any of the parts of the Elephant. On his command, one of Mr. Yeaman's servants produced a musket;
which he primed with great ostentation, and proceeded to
fire into the air, to the mortal injury of a passing gull, and
the severe shock of the assembled people. With a last wail
the gull plunged like a brilliant from the blue sky, to be set
upon by a furious pack of dogs, whose lust for prey had
been excited beyond discipline by the smell of the dead
Elephant; the crowd retired grumbling to a safe distance
and called out insults to Yeaman's men.

Curiously, as the people stepped back, so the
Elephant, exposed upon its watery death-bed, seemed
to grow smaller. In the centre of a great crowd, it was

a mountain, a monstrosity. Against the flat fields by the
Tay, it appeared less significant, hacked, wrinkled, filthy,
sad, abandoned.

The common people having been cleared from his
path, Dr. Blair then approached the animal; it was evident
that the flame of the brute had long been extinguished
in the oily waters of the ditch. But now the Light of
Philosophy shone brightly in the surgeon's eye, and he
gave me my instructions: "I will conduct a philosophical
investigation of this animal's anatomy. You are to attend
to me day or night for the next week or as long as it takes
me to dissect, catalogue and draw the animal. You will, as
usual, be rewarded handsomely," said he, without a trace
of irony. "All I expect is your common skill." With that,
he turned away, expecting that I would be grateful for the
commission.

I knew at that moment that, if indeed this was an
Elephant, it was my duty to record this day and all subsequent days for my children. This is perhaps the most
significant Adventure in the history of Dundee. And I am
a part of it.

———•———

Before us lay the vast stinking corpse, already rank under
the beating sun, giving off odours worse than any charnel-
house; of which, I confess, I have encountered several,
Dr. Blair being a great frequenter of such places with his
engraver, delighting in the glaur and gore of the slain and
the unfortunate. There could be no delay, either, since at
every moment, the country people were poised to rush
back into their butchery, sweeping aside the instruments
and agents of Philosophical Discovery; indeed, once Mr.

Yeaman had ordered his pelt, the magistrate himself was
eager to abandon the spot and only with a great show of
trouble did he leave behind a man as a guard for Dr. Blair.
His words, which I record below, were unbecoming for
a man in his dignified position, and not calculated to advance the cause of his elevation to Provost of the town:
"Blair," said he, smiling the while upon the crowd, "your
undoubted philosophical and surgical skills give you
a right to my admiration; but give you no claim on my
protection; I have the pelt, you have the meat and bones
– what more can you desire?"

To which question, Dr. Blair had no response. This
is a wonder in itself, for Dr. Patrick Blair is a man who
would repulse the wildest cannibal with words alone.

We stepped up to the dead monster, with strong
intentions of business, but fearful that, at any moment,
it might raise its head and smite us down. One stroke
from its nose would have felled us, surely. But it did not
move. For the next several hours, I was obliged to stain
my clothes in crouching down amongst the flayed flesh
and stinking entrails; to record on my paper such items
of great interest as Dr. Blair pointed out to me, the sweat
from my brow sucked by a thousand thousand flies, all
those of the valley of the Tay which had gathered around
us for to feast. The butchers for their part, were disin-
clined to listen to any advice that Dr. Blair offered them,
exercising their time-sharpened skills in the only manner they knew how. Dr. Blair could not persuade them
to look upon the carcass with the eyes of Philosophers.
"The Eighteenth Century", he had told me once, during
one of his many sermons on the Rationality of Man, "is
the epoch of Philosophy and Study, the time in which we

shall lay bare the inner-most mechanisms designed by the Great Author of Nature. It is our duty to manifest the Glory of God and his Omnipotence in endowing Man with a rational faculty to discern those wonderful pro- ductions of his divine Wisdom." The butchers of Dundee have yet to fully understand the Eighteenth Century and the Rational Faculty; but were as anxious as Dr. Blair to complete the job before the Sabbath.[6]

While Dr. Blair supervised the extraction of large and bloodied masses of the Elephant's inner parts, it was left to his mutinous butchers, ably assisted by my- self, whose hair became engorged with clots and gore, to perform the necessary incisions. In an act of Christian sympathy for the departed, Mr. Stuart Potter, piper of the Kirkgate, had taken up a position on an eminence of the road, and played long and hard at several laments, which much calmed the passions of the day; and earned him both weary curses and pennies. For his part, Blair stood upon his carriage, so as to obtain, as he explained, the "optimal supervision" of the body; already a tall man, he stood above the whole scene, much as a general must stand above his army. Unintentionally perhaps, he also stood down-wind and well away from the rising stench of the corpse and its attendant flies. This I ad- mire solely in the man: he has a keen eye for the parts of the body, perhaps equalled only by the trained eye of

---

6. Dr. Blair's statement, made at the start of last century, is remarkable for its perspicuity; we all recognize now the astounding advances made in Science, frequently by Britons of Dr. Blair's learning and character. How much more do we know now, barely a hundred years later, and how little is there left for us to discover!

a master-butcher. While we hacked at mounds of flesh and intestine, he correctly – or so it seemed – guided our hands and our blades.

Dr. Blair directed us to open the abdomen; no sooner had a slit been cut with a ready knife, than a huge mass of slithering, bloody guts and intestine shot out upon us, and covered the ground; my boots were immersed in the horror; men turned pale; Mr. Potter's pipes faltered; Dr. Blair merely looked annoyed with us, and urged us to work faster. One by one, we pulled out from the chaotic mass the heavy *Liver*, the unmentionable *Uterus*, and the *Bladder*, over which last two items the butchers shook their heads in sheer puzzlement, seeing no reason for a man of Dr. Blair's standing to be troubled with such trip-ery. I believe that they did not wilfully mis-understand his intentions: in truth, they believed that Dr. Blair was preparing some Hedonistical feast for the great and wor-thy of Dundee, or perhaps some political breakfast in the cause of Mr. Yeaman.

Great murmurs of appreciation arose, however, when Dr. Blair commanded that the head be detached from the body and brought up to the road; here indeed, in the eyes of all assembled, looked to be a feast of true delight – many a man of Dundee appreciates his 'potted heid'.[7]

---

7. In this, if in nothing else in his Journal, Mr. Orum is correct: 'Potted Heid' remains a dish of great *Epicurean* relish and one which our late wife prepared for our supper every third Saturday of the month.

But let me reveal this: in the course of this long and stinking afternoon, it became evident that one significant part
of the Elephant was missing; without a doubt, an early
butcher had made off with the left fore-foot. How the thief
had managed this in brightest day-light without coming
to the attention of Mr. Yeaman or Dr. Blair, is beyond
comprehension, since its gigantic dimensions – judging
by its twin, the right fore-foot – forbade concealment
under a coat or shawl. Whither it had been taken was unknown – upon discovery of the theft as we laboured at the
high road, Dr. Blair had glared in righteous disapproba-
tion at the cottages in the fields around, and sucked at his
lower lip, but neither cottages nor cotters were quailed by
this demonstration of Affronted Philosophy. There was
nothing to be done for the instant about the loss; and this
was the only theft, apart from some inconsiderable meaty
portions of no great concern to Dr. Blair.[8]

With the arrival of the night, Mr. Potter put away his
pipes, to the great applause of everyone present, torches
were lit, and the items which Dr. Blair proposed to trans-
port back to Dundee were placed upon straw in a wagon
hired from a fortunate carter. Dr. Blair then led the way
homewards in his carriage, while I was relegated to the
post of postilion on the executioner's cart which bore the
Elephant's Head. What a seat I had, what a view! The

---

8. It is a sad fact that the common people, uneducated and
apparently untouched by Christian Propriety, will appropriate to
themselves that which belongs to others. Nevertheless, Mr. Orum
reveals that the people of Dundee are perhaps more honest than
most: how much of the Elephant would have remained in the fields
for our Philosopher had it died, say, in Aberdeen, or Edinburgh?

head was beyond comprehension – by itself, it was even
larger than a cow. I remained dumb with admiration at
the Works of God. Behind us in the gloom as we left, I
could hear the stealthy stirring and hooting of the country people, as they came to examine the mortal remains,
with little or no regard for the memory of that unfortunate
animal. We soon reached the town, and came at last to the
back yard of Dr. Blair's house on Crichton-street; the doctor had given orders that the subjects of his anatomical
enquiries were to be stored temporarily in the kitchen.

Unfortunately, he had not informed his cook. Who, on
turning from her pots, was confronted by a dis-embodied
Elephant's head forcing its irresistible way into her kitch-
en; I, at least, had had the time to grow accustomed to the
strange and unsettling object; the poor woman believed
on the instant that her nightmares had taken living form,
that all the creatures of Hell were now emerging from
the pit and coming to assail her in her own domain. She
screamed wildly and hurled Dr. Blair's supper at the
Head, following this missile with a stream of curses, before swooning to the floor. The Head came on, turning
this way and that, seeming to search out its prey – but
in reality trying to squeeze its uncommon width through
the narrow door-way. Since no one else seemed greatly
discomfited by the cook's incapacity; and since those who
might, were generally encumbered by large pieces of viscera; and those who should, seemed not at all disturbed;
it fell to me, covered in the outward signs of carnage as
I was, to care for the disappointed lady. Having no easy
access to salts, I slapped her gently about the cheeks until
she opened her eyes; but I fear that my appearance was
unlooked-for, since she shrieked twice as loudly as before,

convinced that she was being carried off by a Demon, and belaboured me with her fists. She was a strong woman, and her language was a match: "Do not touch my ****, you ******* ****!!", she cried. Such language made me recoil in horror, with the result that she fell again to the slippery floor; while I for my part cannoned like spittle on hot iron from *Liver* to Cook to *Kidneys* in swift succession; before being propelled head-first into the mass of flesh and bone that was the base of the neck; my hands plunged deep into dead meat, my head embedded for the moment within its skull.

At last, however, the arrangements for the storage of the precious items were completed, and the kitchen emptied of all save the furious cursing cook. I was pitched out into the street to make my way homewards as best I could. The night was dark, but mild. I felt the sticky clinging bloods of the Elephant about my person; my hair was in a state of grumous disarray, my hands black, my clothes stank of drying offal and the rank bodily fluids of the beast. On my short road home, I encountered several Dundee worthies abroad, about their own business; but to my surprise, none of them remarked upon my appearance or recoiled at the offensive stench. What different response might I have met with in Perth, or Edinburgh, or the bright streets of London! Despite this, I felt shame cling to me like a shroud, tripping my feet, inhibiting my arms, blinding my eyes, so that I staggered from close to close, corner to corner.

Not far from Dr. Blair's house, I came across two figures slumped against a wall, muttering incomprehensibly, arms around each others' shoulders, a sad embrace common to a Saturday night in these parts, an embrace broken only by the dawn of the Sabbath or the arrival of an enraged wife. As I crept past the two forms, one of them called out. *"Senhor!"* I turned, and made out the faces of the Elephant's owner and his assistant, both far advanced in their Mourning. The elder of the two stood up unsteadily and introduced himself as '*Senhor Santos*', and his assistant as '*Giovanni*'. Mr. Santos was, he said, a native of Portugal; notwithstanding which poor beginning, he spoke English as well as, and possibly better than, many of the claimant and pretending Kings of Great Britain.[9] Giovanni spoke no English, but was well-versed in the language of the Elephant.

After our introductions were complete, Mr. Santos asked of me: "What have they done to my Elephant?"; he gave me to understand that its name was *Florentia*. I saw no reason to upset the man any more than he already was, so I informed him simply that the Elephant was now taken care of, and that it was in God's Hands, which is all that could be asked for. Mr. Santos, clearly a man of some moral understanding, was content with such a commonplace, although Giovanni continued to wail quietly to himself and curse, as I understood it, the butchering ways of the English.[10]

---

9. This irrational and disloyal remark should, it goes without saying, not be seen to reflect on our dearly-loved and lately-departed King George IV.

10. We find that foreigners commonly mistake Scotchmen for Englishmen. But since the Act of Union was passed by both Parliaments within the following year, our Italian friend should more properly have commented upon 'butchering *Great-Britons*', neither Scotch nor English.

"But what will you do now?" I asked them, concerned for their simple needs, now that they were far from their home, without means of generating a steady income. The Portuguese gentleman assured me that he had enough in his purse to see them safely home and thanked me for my concern; overcome by a sense of charity, I asked them if they wished to sleep in our room that night, before they departed for the south. They were pleased to accept my Samaritan offer.

My arrival at such a late hour, in the company of two foreign gentlemen, was met with the unlimited distraction of my wife Hellen; the terrified silence of my three children, who have been taught by experience naturally to expect the worst from every unforeseen incident; and an outburst of indignation from my mother; for my room is but small even for the six of us to live in, and scarce fitted for two further guests. My wife tenderly pointed out to me that I was covered from head to foot in dried gobbets of blood, my face cob-webbed with sticky sinew, that my boots were caked in a gluey mass of mud and fat, my hair was plastered down with putrefying ooze. As we adopted measures to cleanse myself of the marks of the day with ample use of hot water, my mother subjected my two new friends to questions; to the ever greater confusion of all three of them. At last, unable to understand the presence of two foreign gentlemen of pleasing and refined aspect, she threw herself into a noisy fit of rage such as we had frequently witnessed before. The scene was not improved by Giovanni's decision, finding himself in a Scotch Chamber of Howling, to howl loudly for the loss of his Elephant; and in no time at all the stair was filled with sympathetic neighbours; who, in their turn, gave voice to their inner-most feelings. But within the passage of an hour, to the relief of all, peace had been restored.

My three children, who on other nights sleep safely under the table, shrouded by a cloth, have been chased from their nest, and placed in my wife's bed. Giovanni finds it comfortable to sleep upon the table-top, while Mr. Santos stretches himself out underneath.

28 APRIL 1706.

I awoke early this morning, still seated at the table, my head resting on the first pages of my new Journal. I discovered, when I rubbed my eyes of sleep, that my horn of ink had tipped over in the night and stained the upper body of Giovanni; fortunately, no damage had been done to my papers. Moreover, my feet, so comfortably rested upon Mr. Santos, had been gripped by that strong man between his thighs in a manner that was far from decent, permitting me a more-than-intimate insight into his dreams. Carefully, so as not to excite the passions of a foreigner, I extricated my feet from their warm den, removed my pen, papers and ink-horn and all evidence of my nocturnal labours, then lay down beside my family for two hours of proper sleep.

We were waked at length by a wail from Giovanni, upon his sudden discovery that his chest had turned black in the night. Mr. Santos, who by contrast had turned extremely pale, feared that the young man had contracted the Plague. Naturally, this fear consumed my mother and my children and caused an uproar. It was no great surprise when several of my neighbours arrived at our door, to voice their complaints; on hearing my mother proclaim proudly that the Plague was upon our house, they soon retired to a safe distance. Within minutes, despite my attempts to explain the accident, Dr. Patrick Blair was summoned, to determine for himself what measures should be taken to contain the outbreak of the dread sickness; on examining the patient more closely, he shook his head sombrely and pronounced his opinion: *Pestilentia*

Atramenti. Giovanni, on hearing the word for pestilence, tore at his hair in impassioned despair; and was not to be calmed until the surgeon demonstrated how the disease was caught.[11]

My wife having supplied Giovanni with a clean shirt, and soaked his inky one in a basin, we attended to the matters of the day. My family attended the Sabbath service and sermon of the Reverend Mr. James Robertson in the Dens Kirk. Mr. Santos and the inconsolable Giovanni, while not firm adherents of the Scottish Kirk, asked to accompany us, downcast, no doubt, by their sudden loss. My mother was also brought along, for, although she infrequently attended to any of the words of Christian worship, she liked to be among enthusing crowds. Mr. Robertson is a man of considerable piety, being an admirer – in private, if not in the pulpit – of the very saintly Richard Cameron.[12] He endeavours to draw spiritual lessons directly from 'whatever is new'; for him, as for many of us in Dundee, much that is 'new' is a confirmation of the sinfulness of men – and what could be more 'new' that day than the arrival of the Elephant from

---

11. It is pleasing to see that our fellow-citizens of Ancient Dundee took such sensible precautions immediately upon learning of the infection. Dr. Blair is to be praised for his rapid and selfless engagement in the case; no such praise may be bestowed upon Mr. Orum, who reveals himself here – and not for the last time – as a fool.

12. Mr. Richard Cameron was he who founded the Cameronian Sect of deluded Radicals, the infamous 'Lion of the Covenant', justly executed for his pernicious views in the year 1680. Whether Mr. Robertson was indeed an adherent of the Cameronians, as Mr. Orum claims, is a matter of conjecture.

Broughty Ferry and the welcome afforded it by the people of Dundee?

Accordingly, he set to with enthusiasm unfettered, and we were uplifted by the words of Job, Chapter 40, and Esdras, Chapter 6, wherein the Behemoth and the Leviathan are discussed – "Behold now Behemoth," announced Mr. Robertson, in a mighty voice; so mighty on this day that many in the congregation sat up straight in their seats as a body and gazed around them in holy terror, expecting to see the dead Elephant brought back to life and rampaging down the aisle towards them; "Lo now, his strength is in his loins and his force is in the navel of his belly!" At these words, my mother, unable to contain her demons, laughed long and loud, to the very great chagrin of my wife and my three children. Mr. Robertson, rather than being angry, welcomed the interruption; for he is a man of great religious clarity, and has many times told me that my mother was possessed by the Spirit; and continued with a description of the Behemoth which seemed far removed from the sad sight which lay before us yesterday – "He moveth his tail like a cedar: the sinews of his stones are wrapped together. His bones are as strong pieces of brass; his bones are like the bars of iron. He is the chief of the ways of God"; and more.

"Chief of the ways of God": these words resound in my ears. This Elephant, of whose existence I had no knowledge until the preceding day, was God's most significant creation. I am, truly, astounded.

When these words were discreetly explained to him in the Italian tongue by Mr. Santos, Giovanni nodded in delighted agreement with the Presbyterian Faith; and then shed tears; so well did the minister describe his sadly-missed *Florentia*. And when Mr. Robertson went on to deliver the words of Esdras, in Chapter 6 of his Second Book, where the Behemoth is said to live in a land "of a thousand hills", the lamentations of Giovanni possessed the rest of the congregation, and soon the kirk resounded with wailing and the beating of breasts and the gnashing of teeth. My mother, greatly satisfied by the wild commotion around her, howled as she had never howled before; then fell into a deep sleep, from which, two hours later, when the service was over, she could scarce be roused. Mr. Robertson, it need not be said, was greatly affected by the reception of his sermon, and preached long and hard thereafter.

After this energetic demonstration of the town's grief, we returned to our room, and my wife served up some soup; during the meal, Mr. Santos showed himself to be not merely a master of Elephants, but a fountain of much natural knowledge.

"It is probable," proposed Mr. Santos, "that some writers have confused the Elephant and the Hippopotamus, for both are mighty creatures." I knew until today but little of the Hippopotamus, imagining it perhaps to be a magical horse with curative powers; but our Portuguese had seen one of these also in his travels, and had even intended to bring one to Dundee along with the Elephant: alas, he had been unable to do so, since the creature perished; having escaped from a travelling fair, it ascended the smoking slopes of the volcano Vesuvius in Italy and pitched itself headlong into a blazing fissure. Giovanni, understanding what was being discussed in our conversation, launched into some violent diatribe in his own language; the burden of which, explained to me later, was that no heat-loving

creature should evermore be brought to the dark and wet
lands of the north, there to sicken and die, far from the
blue skies and warm waters of its home.

Dr. Blair, had he been at our simple meal, would
doubtless have been enthused at the prospect of another
exotical creature expiring by the banks of the River Tay,
for the singular and precise purpose of allowing him, the
Apothecary-Surgeon, to extend his intimate knowledge of
the internal organs and brass bones of the various wonders of Creation.[13] Dr. Blair is a man who will stop at
nothing, neither hold back from insulting everyone, in
his dark quest for Philosophy and Knowledge. On frequent occasions, this darkness drives him to saw up the
small broken bodies of dead children, scarcely cold, their
grieving parents having been pushed out of the door. He
is a man dancing to the tune of melancholy and sinful
pipes.[14]

As the afternoon drew on, Mr. Santos told me of
ever stranger creatures that he had observed in his travels in the lands around the Mediterranean Sea – the
Rhinoceros, the Giraffe, the Phoenix, the Chamel, the
Flamingo, and other sports of Nature. Some of his tales I

---

13. Dr. Blair's catalogue of animals which he had dissected
was, we are assured by Mr. W.B. of Boston, very considerable: a
horse, a sheep, a porpoise, small children under the age of seven,
larger children up to the age of fourteen, a seal, an otter, a calf. A
Hippopotamus is not, despite Mr. Orum's bold assertions, among
these.

14. In Science, as in Politics, that which is *Unpopular* will
sometimes become *Necessary*. Mr. Orum interprets this as a sin. We
need not reply.

could scarce believe; but I am not a man who has travelled much, and can not be expected to know of the variety of the brutal form. My children sat in a corner and hugged each other for protection as each new wonder was told. My mother, although now returned to her bed for the day, insisted that we speak loudly, that she might listen in on the discussion, and every so often she would let out a howl of emotion – whether of terror, enthusiasm, wonder, or mockery, was sometimes difficult to determine.

At two o'clock, Giovanni sprang up from his doleful corner, donned his damp and inky shirt, and announced that he would visit the place where his beloved Elephant had died, before, as was now planned, embarking upon the journey back to the south. Mr. Santos was unwilling to let Giovanni go on this pilgrimage alone, for fear of what might happen either to him or to the plundering natives; for my part, I was inclined to accompany them; my wife Hellen thought that our three children should go "for some fresh air"; the children had a strong opin⁄ion at variance with this proposal; I conceded that the air might not be at all fresh. At this moment of indecision, seven of my brother Hendrie's children arrived, anxious for some play; and the matter was resolved; we all set off – Giovanni exciting Hendrie's children to ever⁄greater outrages against the Sabbath; Mr. Santos and myself walking in measured pace and earnest discussion; my own children keeping close in my shadow, trembling lest the earth might gush forth fire and lava under their feet. On the road, which was short, but thronged unusually by many people walking in the same direction, Mr. Santos advised me that, though the years of the Elephant be long – some say one hundred or two hundred years – the time

of *Florentia's* years was but eight-and-twenty. "Ah! one
so young!," said I, full of tears and ready sympathy; for
it was at eight-and-twenty years of age also that my first
wife Barbra had died, scarce two weeks after our wedding-
day.

As we strolled down to the high-road, Mr. Santos was
kind enough to provide for me much of the Elephant's
history. The night has reached silence, but I will take the
time to set it down as he told me it.

It had arrived in Mr. Santos's care as part of a com-
plex trade which he undertook in Marseille with some
merchants from Venice, in November of the year 1688.[15]
(The Portuguese gentleman seemed reluctant to impart
details of this trade, though I pressed him hard on the
matter. All that he would tell me was that, as part of the
agreement, his unmarried sister was persuaded to leave
Marseille to seek a new life in Araby.)

For a number of years, Mr. Santos toured the southern
kingdoms of Europe with the Elephant, teaching it many
miraculous tricks and displaying it before both peasant
and prince. In November of the year 1700,[16] Mr. Santos
departed for Madrid in the highest expectation of large
profits to be made from a people whose celebration of
their King's death was profligate; on this journey, he was
now accompanied by young Giovanni who had met up
with, and acquired a deep affection for, the Elephant in

---

15. By the strangest of coincidences, this was the very month that
William of Orange arrived on the shores of England.

16. Curious to relate, this was the very month in which King
Charles II of Spain died. It seems that the fate of our Elephant was
intimately connected with the greatest affairs of State!

the town of Florence, after which the beast was named
Florentia.

In Spain, even in a year of mourning, Elephants are
not so remarkable as they are here in Scotland; and the
commercial profits returned from fair-ground appear-
ances and performances were but poor. The journey was
therefore continued onward to Portugal, where matters
barely improved; after some years of "drought and fam-
ine", as he expressed it, Mr. Santos boarded a ship car-
rying port-wine from Porto to England, in August of the
year 1704.[17] The crossing of the sea being very rough and
perilous, the Elephant was greatly terrified; and all were
relieved to reach the port of Torbay safely. Mr. Santos
then made his way into the country towns and villages
where the Elephant, now completely recovered from her
ordeals, provided a grand spectacle.

Throughout the year 1705, the Elephant toured the
lower parts of the Queen's Realm, and Mr. Santos was
able to increase his profits so rapidly as to buy himself
a carriage; which the Elephant pulled from town to
town, Giovanni sitting upon her mighty shoulder, the
Portuguese on cushions within the carriage. Alas for
Man's Arrogance! – upon the Elephant's approach to
the town of Carlisle in February of 1706, the Almighty
sent down a great storm and swept the carriage into the
river, to Mr. Santos's great peril. He was saved only by
the wit of the Elephant, which thrust out her remarkable
nose upon the waters for the drowning man to clutch. All

17. Our Readers will need no reminder that this was the precise
year and month in which Sir George Rooke took possession of the
island of Gibraltar as a British possession in perpetuity.

of their possessions and moneys were lost beneath the turgid torrents.

Beginning anew, therefore, the travellers fetched up in Kirkcudbright, Dumfries, Ayr, and many smaller places in the south of Scotland; arriving finally in Edinburgh where a fortune might be expected from the provision of Elephantine entertainment; and where expectations were soon disappointed, the citizens of Edinburgh being weary of novelties and overly canny with their purses.[18] However, the exhibitions in Edinburgh attracted the notice of certain Lords of Scotland as they gathered to debate the proposed Union; and Mr. Santos was invited with Elephant to the palace of the Duchess of Hamilton, to parade the Elephant before Her Grace, and, as he told me with the greatest pride, to have her perform many goodly and amusing tricks. (He referred, lest I be misunderstood, to the tricks of the Elephant, not of the Duchess.) The Duchess was greatly entertained, reported my Portuguese friend, and rewarded him with two guineas, and Giovanni with a dollar, a most generous payment for such a brief display of the Elephant's endowments. The noble animal, for its troubles, received a soft bed for the night in a storehouse full of hay, sleeping soundly between her owner and her attendant. Did he not, I asked Mr. Santos, feel fear to sleep so close to such a large mass of brutal flesh; was he not troubled at the thought of being

---

18. Alas! – Mr. Santos's observation was only too accurate. We ourselves refuse to take the coach to Edinburgh, knowing full well that a gentleman will soon be separated from his wealth, his honour and his reputation, with nothing to show for the loss, once he sets foot upon those gilded streets.

suffocated or crushed under its massive weight? Not at all, said my new friend, for the Elephant is a most careful and tender creature among those of God's Creation. I observed to Mr. Santos that the Elephant was indeed "the chief of the ways of God"; he concurred gravely.

After leaving the Palace of Hamilton at the beginning of this month, the travellers proceeded northwards, recommended to the Duke of Argyle at his palace; where, Mr. Santos proudly told me, the animal industriously cleaned a stable, sorting clean straw from dunged straw and consuming great amounts of the former – a remarkable performance worthy of record, indicating the intelligence of the beast; but not, it seems, raising it much in the estimation of the Duke's stableman. What is most remarkable about this further journey into the North is that the Elephant was able to march so many miles across our country in so few days. Within a fortnight of leaving Hamilton, the party had arrived in the cold blasted town of Aberdeen where the inhabitants regarded the entertainment with less enthusiasm than most.

Mr. Santos confessed to me that he did not understand the citizens of that town, "tho' he had seen more of Man than many another"; for they seemed at once suspicious and credulous, both miserly and extravagant; after several, more worthy, demonstrations of the Elephant's sympathetic nature had been greeted with a stony silence, it took but one worthless trick of the Elephant, that of delicately removing the wig of an inebriated doctor of the university and placing it upon the top of a bare tree, for the audience to turn from a sullen crowd of passers-by to a delighted, raucous, riotous assemblage. That night, a generous farmer offered his accommodations to the party.

But the Elephant, feeling hungry and scenting bags of corn in an adjacent part of the building, tried to enter the store-room through a narrow door; became wedged, and broke down the door entirely; then consumed several pecks of the grain. Fearing for his liberty, Mr. Santos fled across the River Dee; and arrived in Broughty Ferry, on the 26th day of April. The weather being clear and hot, they gave one performance of the Elephant's skills in the main street of Broughty Ferry. Much to Mr. Santos's discomfiture, the greatest entertainment of all for these people was the size of the turds of the Elephant, which excited expressions of awe and disbelief.

On the following day, the travellers marched from our neighbouring town to Dundee, in hopes of great profit.

Alas! for the Elephant *Florentia*, and for the sanity and well-being of Giovanni, she did not reach Dundee alive! Coming within a mile of the town upon the coast-road, the Elephant suddenly sat upon her hind legs, sighed deeply, then lay down upon her side at the edge of the road. Giovanni had been upon her shoulders, as was usual, and narrowly escaped being crushed by her precipitate decline. For several hours, in the great heat of the day, her Keeper and her Owner endeavoured, with the assistance of some country-people, to raise the beast to her feet again. Their attempts met with no success at all. By evening, it was evident that the animal would be obliged to spend the night there; so *Senhor* Santos caused a ditch to be dug around her, that she might lie more easily, with her feet below the rest of her tired body. "A remarkable ditch, *Senhor* Orum", he told me, "it cost me four shillings Scots."[19]

But by a catastrophical mis-chance, this ditch proved

to be her grave: for in the night, despite the heat and cloudless aspect of all the days before and after, the skies poured down rain such as we usually experience in the month of February. Within the hours of darkness, the ditch filled with water; and, when the sun rose the following day, Saturday the 27th day of April 1706, the Elephant had been drowned in the ditch.

"Mr. Orum," said Mr. Santos with tears welling from his eyes, "I do not know how it is in your great country when an animal dies. But, to avoid possible imprisonment as the final insult to Fate's cruel trick, I made haste to find an honest magistrate of your town, to record the creature's death, and to swear on oath that we made no designed injury upon her." I assured him that in Scotland, there was no great concern should a man kill his dog, his horse, or – should he be of comfortable means – even some common labourer; that the finding of an honest magistrate would be a lucky chance indeed; and that in any case his fears were likely groundless. Nonetheless, the report had been made; a certificate of doubtful value was issued; and Mr. Yeaman, ever one to make profit from the misfortunes of others, made haste to secure for himself the corpse of the deceased as it lay in a ditch in indignity.[20]

---

19. Four shillings Scots for a ditch is a small price to pay, we would argue, for the comfort of such a large beast. It seems that our *Continental* friends are less generous than they would have us believe, when they repeat their humorous anecdotes about 'mean Scotchmen'.

20. In this paragraph, Mr. Orum reveals his true, odious character. Not content with impugning the good, solid virtues of all decent

As Senhor Santos talked, we reached the place of *Florentia's* demise: the scene was lively. From far and wide, the people of the Tay had gathered, some to pay their last respects to the huge beast. Other people had ar- rived upon the painful scene, bearing baskets and pushing wheel-barrows, hoping to make off with some morsel for supper; but were restrained in the execution of their plan by those who came merely to observe. Such conflicting notions as to the proper way of welcoming the bounty of Nature gave rise to numberless arguments. Mr. Santos being recognized as the moral owner of the remains, now lively with flies, he was permitted to pass through the jostling crowd to the last resting-place; where, with Portuguese hat in hand, he said a silent prayer or two. Giovanni, as was to be expected, was not slow to show his own sorrow, striking his jet-black hair into wild peaks and waves, and uttering Italian words of keenest grief; whereby he excited considerable sympathy in the matrons and unattached females around him, who gave enthusiastic applause to his handsome ways. At length, we turned back: the two travellers intended to set off on their southwards journey without delay. Before they left, Mr. Santos shook my hand warmly, but in great sorrow.

"*Florentia* was," he said, wiping the tears from his eyes with a copious black cloth, "the *ultimo* Elephant. You un- derstand, *Senhor* Orum: *ultimo*?"

I looked blankly at him. In despair, Mr. Santos called

Britons, whose possessions, we would add, are their own, he slanders Mr. Yeaman, for whom personal profit and material gain were quite repugnant – he became, after all, a Member of Parliament – and whose rectitude in matters of business was proverbial.

upon Giovanni; there was a hurried conversation between them; Giovanni cast his huge dark eyes upon me and re peated dolefully: "*Ultimo, ultimo.*"

I puzzled over this, long after the two men had dis appeared into the sun that set over Perth; but I believe I now understand: *ultimo* – ultimate – the Last One. It is long since a wolf was seen in Scotland – men say the Last Wolf was killed some years ago. Do we stand now, in 1706, at the edge of a precipice, in which all of God's creatures will be killed off, one by one, dissected perhaps by Dr. Blair and then cast aside? Is it not our duty as sin ners seeking forgiveness, to ensure that the ways of God are preserved? Is this Last Elephant the first of the Last Ones?[21] I tremble: the night is cold and endless. My dear wife cannot keep me warm.

---

21. It is not at all certain either what Mr. Santos intended, or that Mr. Orum understood. It was not the last Elephant, for we are advised by everyone with whom we have corresponded, and especially those who have served our interests in *India*, that Elephants continue to roam the world in vast numbers. No more can it have been the last Elephant than it could have been the last Tiger, or the last Whale. Did Mr. Santos perhaps intend to say that this was the "Last Elephant" which he would own? We cannot tell, nor is Mr. Santos with us to explain in plain English what he meant. So much for Foreigners.

29 APRIL 1706.

It was with considerable bleakness of mood that I awoke this morning. I had not slept well, I felt an emptiness in me. But, having been instructed, on the Saturday night as I was sent home, to attend Dr. Blair at first light on the Monday morning, I made haste to visit the shops to acquire, without the benefit of coin, such small items of food and drink as my family required. You will not be surprised to learn that these purchases were made only with the greatest difficulty, and that I fled each shop under a torrent of abuse, being advised by one trader after another that I need not bother them again until I had paid off all my debts.[22] In the greatest of haste, and having no time to eat, I abandoned my family, and ran with all the instruments of my profession to the house of Dr. Blair.

I found that I need not have brought any of the instruments of my profession; what Dr. Blair required most that day, he announced, were the arms and legs of a dozen strong men. I tried to excuse myself from whatever task he had in mind; but he merely dismissed my concerns, and placed me under orders as one of the foot-soldiers in his War of Philosophy against Ignorance. Without further ado, we advanced in a small battalion: all loaded aboard two rough carts were myself, Mr. Menteith, and

---

22. We need only note Mr. Orum's shameless record of indebtedness to assess his true character. No man should – as we never have – fall into debt with tradesmen. Debt leads to Poverty, Poverty to Immorality, Immorality to Depravity, Depravity once more to Debt.

a band of perhaps half-a-dozen uncouth porters from the harbour; we were preceded by Dr. Blair in one carriage, accompanied by a number of his surgical students; and a second carriage containing a *'Squadrone Volante'* – as Dr. Blair joked, describing his own carriage-load, equally obscurely, as the *'Country Party'*[23] – of the other Physicians of Dundee; the whole forming a procession much as if we were all on some festival outing. A festival it was not to be, unless it had been a Festival of Carnage; for our philosophical leader took us as far as the last resting-place of the Elephant, with which I was becoming more than enough familiar; and we were given our orders, which were to obtain full possession of the remaining parts of the Elephant's corpse and return with them to Dundee.

The day was clear and hot, despite a breeze: Dr. Blair lamented that the heat of the preceding days had dried out the intestines, so that he would have no opportunity of investigating them in any detail; the rest of us lamented the flies and the stench, that gave us no opportunity of drawing a breath of fresh air. Around us as we laboured, Dr. Blair's students and fellow-physicians cut and sawed. I could see that the skills of slicing and sawing were no better among the physicians than among the butchers whose crudeness Dr. Blair had so rebuked on the Saturday; as for his students, the skills were utterly lacking. I thought with some horror of the possibility of suffering an injury and being ministered to by the shaking hand of some such

---

23. Dr. Blair's humorous references are, of course, to two of the Political parties engaged at that time in the debate around the Act of Union. Mr. Orum, having little education, could not be expected to understand this.

young apprentice; and guarded myself very carefully lest some accident befall me, either through a slip of my foot – I was greatly exhausted from a lack of sleep – or through a slip of their knives.

Throughout these long hours, Dr. Blair stood – as before – high above us. His wig, driven by enthusiasm, slipped backwards over his strong forehead. With his cane, which he used to support his bad leg, he directed every cut. The loathsome Menteith was sent forth every two minutes with some detailed instruction for one of the army of butchers; he darted through the crowd, and bel-lowed that instruction in the ear of a student or a doctor or a butcher; then he strutted back to resume his posi-tion up beside his master, dark, narrow-eyed, his features screwed in an assumed importance that was never his. At the end of that day, we had two wagons loaded with all that remained of the Elephant – excepting of course one foot; these were despatched to Dr. Blair's back-door. No great artistry had been used in loading the wagon, and various indistinct parts of the sad Elephant lay heavily on other parts, in no way that the Almighty could have designed. On arrival at the house, our final task was to unload the various stinking and sordid items and to store them, as directed, in Dr. Blair's various out-houses; or, much to the disgust of the cook, in piles in the kitchen, already full to overflowing with pieces of the Head.

"Never mind, Miss Gloag!" shouted the doctor, dis-regarding – indeed, encouraged by – the cook's robust protestations, "Just think that your splendid kitchen has this evening played a part in the History of Philosophical Experiment!"

Miss Gloag expressed her ardent desire that Philo-

sophical Experiment would rot slowly from its **** upwards, die painfully, and be ****** by Satan forever. At
this powerful curse, Dr. Blair merely laughed: in this display of courage alone, I confess, I admire him, for I myself
would not be the man to thwart the cook. But – he was the
master, she but the servant – as were we all that day.

After two hours of hard labour, the remaining anatomical pieces of the Elephant were secure within Dr. Blair's
policies; the wagons, stinking of carnage, were driven off
to be washed down; and the hired hands, malodorous,
disappeared into the gloom; I made my way homewards,
to record the events of the day in my new Journal and try
to sleep.

Sleep evades me. My candle has long since extinguished, and all I can think of is Death: the age of an
Elephant; the age of Man; the age of Woman. Three-
score and ten is considered the usual allotted span of our
years. But it seems to me that the age of Man is either
greatly exaggerated, or that it has diminished considerably since the days of the Patriarchs; for the common age
of death among the poorer people of Dundee is perhaps
thirty or forty, by which time the trials and burdens of the
world have taken their toll; a fresh-faced young woman of
eighteen may turn, in a matter of three years of marriage,
child-bearing and daily toil, to a woman of middle years,
haggard, bitter, bowed, lined, grey; a man of thirty will
pass, within a twelve-month, to a white-haired cripple, if
he suffers one of many possible accidents in his labour;
anyone above the age of forty is justly considered to be
both a miracle of longevity and a dribbling idiot. In the
country-side around Dundee, the people fare little better
than in the town – the air is fresher and the cottages less

noxious, but their lives are harder from dawn until dusk.[24]
Only those of the more philosophical trades and profes-
sions, the doctors and lawyers and gentlemen and merchants, live to great ages. My own father, who laboured
his life away in the weaving mill, died at the age of four-
and-thirty, leaving my mother to raise me to manhood; at
which time, seeing her duty done, and her responsibility
carried out, she immediately advanced her years from
eight-and-thirty to eight-and-eighty in one night. Dr.
Patrick Blair, for whom I was then working, and on whom
I called for medical advice at the catastrophe, diagnosed
her illness as a rush of stormy blood which damaged the
senses; I know not. All I know is that, where once she was
my mother, my tormentor and a great trial for a young
man of eighteen years, she had in a single day become to
me an object of pity; I might even call it love, although I
do not know what the word truly means.

The Last Elephant died at the age of eight-and-twenty:
truly, the Days of God's Creations are short.[25]

In the night, when all should be silent; when even my

---

24. Mr. Orum's remarks on the Health of Great-Britons are, of
course, one hundred and more years into the Past. While it can
scarcely be said that the morals and health of our poorer classes
has much improved – a fact that must be attributed to *Intoxicating
Spirits* and *Loose Living* – it is only a matter of time before the
diseases of this world are eradicated.

25. Dr. Blair found the immaturity of this Elephant to have been a
great advantage for his scientific researches. Let us quote from his
Essay:

"She seems to have been Young, according to the Term of Life,
for the Epiphyses separated from the Bones by Boyling as easily, as
those of a Human Subject would have done at the Age of 10 or 12."

mother has abandoned her howls in favour of loud snores;
I stay awake and consider certain matters, which, at my
time of life, are close to my heart. I trust I shall not embarrass myself by revealing that my thoughts turned to:
procreation. We live in an uncertain world. My dear first
wife Barbra died when the flowers of her bridal wreath
had scarce faded; my dearest Hellen has been in one constant condition for several years past – unwell; our first
son Thomas died while still an infant – who can foretell
what might happen to my little children who cling so
helplessly to each other beneath our table? Might they
not of a sudden be taken from us by a sickness or the pox;
and perhaps end up satisfying the philosophical curiosity
of Dr. Blair and his kind? These are thoughts which it is
hard to bear in the darkest night; I tried just now to hold
my wife tightly in my arms, for fear that the name of Orum
would slip away into Oblivion. However, she pushed me
away weakly, complaining that I smell of Elephant; I am
obliged to sit up alone.

I will close this page of my Journal, for some thoughts
which now occur to me should never be expressed.[26]

---

26. We are obliged to your decorum, Mr. Orum! So much for
Procreation.

30 APRIL 1706.

I found myself this morning more dead than alive, perhaps the Last Engraver. Despite my exhaustion from
the drawn-out physical labours of the previous day, I
had sat sleepless like a dead man; and stirred, aching in
every limb, only late in the morning.[27] I dragged myself
from my bed, carried out my paternal responsibilities
and walked as well as I could to the house of Dr. Blair.
I confess that each step I took was a heavy one, a slow
one, for much in my spirit railed against Dr. Blair and his
proposed dissection of the last of the chief of the ways of
God. What could I, a poor sinner, a mere engraver, do to
halt the surgeon's designs?

My late arrival was greeted with disapproval, for it
seemed that the Great Work had already begun: Dr.
Blair was in the kitchen, unaffected by the wrath of his
cook, who uttered the following memorable judgement
of her present situation: "******, *******, ****, *****,
*****"; then smote in amongst her pots and pans while
the doctor began his close examination and measure-
ment of the various items of anatomy, some of which
had lain there since Saturday night. I was instructed to
make drawings of this bloody article, and of that putrefying piece of flesh, after he had extracted them carefully
from the shapeless heap that slowly slithered over the

---

27. Is any further demonstration of Mr. Orum's deficient character
necessary? We are of the strong opinion that "early to bed and early
to rise makes a man healthy, wealthy and wise". Mrs. S., our dear
wife, gave voice to this sound principle on many occasions.

flagstones of the kitchen; and when I had completed my sketch, he would seize a pen and write some Latin name at the foot of the paper and lay the paper to one side. While Dr. Blair took apart God's Creation, piece by piece, I re-constructed it on paper, piece by piece: the battle was engaged. Dr. Blair's excitement and energy was without limit, and I could barely work swiftly enough to keep up with him. He treated me, in this procedure, as if I had no feelings, nor any thoughts; he said nothing to me, merely pulled papers from my hand, then passed them back to me, much as if I had been a statue. When I complained of a certain faintness due to lack of food, he only heaped scorn upon me: "You think of food and drink at such a moment as this, Mr. Orum? I am engaged in one of the most exciting dissections ever performed in this part of Europe, and your stomach rumbles? Fie on you! I have," he continued relentlessly, "spent these last few nights in reading all that has ever been written on Elephants.[28] The natural food of Elephants is grass, and when that is want-ing, they dig up roots with their tusks." As much could also be said of some of our poor country-people, the only difference being, that the country-people have no tusks, making do, in those circumstances, with their bare hands. "They are said," he continued, in his lecture to us, making

---

28. In contrast to Mr. Orum's profligacy, Dr. Blair had spent his evenings wisely. We need no further demonstration of the two opposed characters of our fellow Dundonians – one, who has exalted the name of Dundee by his respected studies and sober life; the other, who brings shame on us, by his mean jealousies and ignorant musings. But – "by Darkness, we may see Light" – shall ever be our Editorial Principle.

our stomachs grumble by the very mention of food, "to have a great delight in cucumbers and melons. When they are tamed, they eat hay, oats, barley, or other such food as oxen and horses eat. An Elephant drinks a great quantity of water, which it sucks up by the trunk, and whenever that's full, it empties it into the mouth. When they are to go to battle, men give them spirituous liquors, such as wine, *&c*, in order to make them drunk and furious." And as much also, apart from the cucumbers and melons and the matter of the trunk, could be said of our own poor people. How remarkable it is that Dr. Blair does not at once see how close the diet of the Elephant resembles that of the very people among whom he lives.[29]

Thus enlightened, we were set to work two times as fast again.

I was finally provided with a wholesome broth at the dinner-hour, which I ate in the company of an enormous and evil-eyed black cat, and a nervous scullery-maid who coped with the world only by twirling round and round at every brief opportunity, and whose ears shone bright red, perhaps from months of hearing the hellish tirades of the cook; both of my companions transfixed me with their eyes throughout the quarter-hour which was spent in this recuperative activity; both seemed profoundly disappointed when I scraped my last spoon-full from the bowl. For all her other faults, there can be no doubt but that the cook makes a good and hearty broth; but she treated

---

29. What outrageous nonsense! The glory of Great Britain is not built upon barley and oats or whisky and rum, but upon a Christian Stalwartness among officers and gentlemen, and Native Ruggedness among men of the poorer classes.

my humble expressions of satisfaction with considerable contempt, using words of which I only dimly understood the scatological meaning.

I cannot tell whether nutritious parts of the Elephant were included in the ingredients of the broth; and did not care to enquire.

———•———

On reaching my home this evening, I found my family in an uproar: my mother was in a howling rage; my children screamed as if the Wee Man himself was after them with his fork, for to press out their little eyes and then saw off their limbs and cast them one by one into a blazing volcano; and my dear wife Hellen had retired to her bed, where she hid her head below the blanket in silence. Outside, several of my neighbours had gathered to demonstrate their concern for my mother and offer words of comfort for my children: "Aye, she'll be dying at last, eh?" and "If ye dinna leather those bairns, ah'll dae it for ye!" I thanked my neighbours for their sympathy; and sought an explanation of the excitement.

It was not far to seek. When I had uncovered my wife, I discovered from her that my brother Hendrie had paid a visit, scarcely an hour since; he had brought with him a basket, which stood now in the middle of our bare table. Hendrie had told them that he thought Mr. Santos would like to have it, as a memento. On being told that Mr. Santos and Giovanni had now left for their home country, Hendrie was puzzled as to what to do; and annoyed that the world had, once again, failed him. "Ah near broke ma back tae get yon," he grumbled; "The magistrate's men were efter my erse!" In the end, he shrugged his shoulders

and indicated that he had best be off, for he had his sup´
per waiting for him; "Gibby will ken fit tae dae wi' it", he
suggested confidently.

After Hendrie's departure, my wife, hoping that it
might contain a present of cloth – for visitors to Dundee
are pleased to take such things away with them, to remind
themselves of their days here – eagerly looked inside the
basket; then threw herself upon the bed, in tears. Agnes,
my eldest and boldest child, then crept up to the basket
and peered inside; she is a child of great sense and ration´
ality, and quickly determined that the basket contained
nothing more nor less than the 'Claw of the Devil.' She
announced this to her brother and sister, who became
greatly agitated; and then to her grand´mother, who
reflected on the implications for several minutes, and
started to howl.

I have looked in the basket to see what it contains. It is,
of course, the left fore´foot of the Last Elephant.

1 MAY 1706.

In the night, as I put my pen down at last and wondered whether sleep would ever return to me, I was visited by the Elephant. She wished to know whether I was firm in my intention to save her from Oblivion. She had an accent to her voice that was similar to that of Mr. Santos. When I assured the Beast that I would not let Dr. Blair alone memorialize her, she nodded sagely with her huge head, but eyed balefully the basket containing her left fore-foot. "Gilbert Orum," she said, "be sure that you do not fail me. For I AM the Ultimate Elephant." With which words she touched me gently with her extraordinary trunk, then turned and descended the stair, trumpeting through her nose as she went, causing my neighbours to wake and to tremble, convinced perhaps that the Last Days had come, as Mr. Robertson has promised they will.

After her departure, I reflected on this: if this was the ultimate, or Last, Elephant, it was my duty as an engraver and a chronicler to ensure that the world knew what the Elephant had looked like, how it moved, how it lived. By contrast, it was Dr. Blair's intention to pull apart, piece by piece, the living beast that once walked cheerfully alongside Mr. Santos and Giovanni. Which of us, I wondered, was in the right? With such thoughts and dreams, I slept but briefly.

The first sight which greeted me as I opened my eyes this morning was that of my three children, sitting in their accustomed place under the table, tears streaming down their cheeks, hiding from the basket which contained the stuff of nightmare. My first task, therefore, was to pay a

visit upon my brother and establish how he had obtained
it. My brother Hendrie lives with his family some hundred steps from us; I arrived at the entrance to the tenement just as he was emerging, blinking, into the sun of the
morning, having been sent out by his wife Margaret, as on
most mornings, to find some small job or task that would
pay money. "Aye, Gibby!" he greeted me enthusiastically,
"Ye'll have got my wee present then, heh? Maggie didna
want it in the hoose, ken?"

I remonstrated with him for the upset he had caused;
but all he did was chastize me for having too timid a family. As he did so, there was a noise as of riotous assembly
and insurrection, and half-a-dozen or so of Hendrie's godless brood came tumbling out of the entrance to the stair,
screaming and kicking at each other and at passers-by;
and disappeared down the close pursued by the cries of
outraged citizens. My brother beamed after them, then
told me proudly of how he had acquired the foot; he had
been down early on the Saturday to the Broughty Ferry
road – "Ah had a wee arrangement wi' Watty – Watty
Fairweather, ken?": such 'arrangements' I knew well,
from Hendrie having been frequently up before the magistrates. I did not enquire into the exact nature of this one
– on the last occasion I had been furnished with details,
I was disappointed to learn that it involved the dung of
cows and a vat of dye used by the weavers at Lochee. The
arrangement with Mr. Fairweather had been frustrated,
as the partner had drunk too much the night before; but
the pair had then come across the tragic scene with the
Elephant at an early hour. Seizing the chance, and an axe
(which had been brought along for their disappointed
project), Hendrie and Watty had made off with the foot,

long before Mr. Yeaman's officers had arrived on the spot.

"A' ah wantit, Gibby," said my brother in a voice that any other might interpret as sincere, "wis tae gie they foreigners a fond wee memory o' their stay in Dundee."[30]

At this moment, my sister-in-law thrust her head from a window above, and told her husband, and the rest of Dundee, that if "he didna shift his erse" straight away, she would hang it out to dry. At the thought of this, Hendrie delayed no longer; he pulled his breeks up tightly and ran off down the close; leaving me with a dilemma.

My first and only duty was to find a new home for the 'Claw of the Devil'; I had no thought to return it to its rightful owner, Dr. Blair; I do not consider him in any case to be the rightful owner – he has, after all, the exciseman's share of the poor beast; he has three of the feet already, and, should the fore-foot be markedly different from the hind-foot, he has the right-most one thereof to satisfy his every desire. But I admit that I had some thought that retaining the foot might bring me profit, spiritual or otherwise.

Returning to our room in haste – for I had to arrive at my station in good time for the day's labour – I did not calmly consider my choices; I seized the basket in both arms; the foot of a dead Elephant being by no means an

---

30. In these more enlightened times, of course, pleasure-seekers will leave Dundee with less disagreeable *mementoes* of our city – a shawl, perhaps, or a good cured fish. We understand that Mr. K. of this town, a maker of confectionery, has great plans for other comestible trinkets to satisfy this passing trade. *Sic tempora, sic mores!*

inconsequential burden; and set off at random into the town, having no plan. Almost immediately, I came up against Miss Speirs, and all but couped her over. Miss Samuella Speirs is the disappointed bridesmaid of my first wife, Barbra. She is always 'after a man'; when Barbra died, Miss Speirs expected that I would turn to her for consolation; I greatly admire Miss Speirs, but I find her robust defiance of peace and quiet to be more than a man can tolerate; and I sought tranquil solace with Hellen Webster instead. In my agitation this morning, I foolishly thought to make use of Samuella's continuing fondness for me, and, having set her upright, asked if she would "keep a wee something for me". She was agreeable and we repaired to the House of Speirs; but, on inspecting my burden within the privacy of the chamber, she swooned – for once speechless; her mother swooned to behold the swooning of her daughter. With both Miss Speirs and Mrs. Speirs lying at my feet, I took the only honourable action that I could in such circumstance; and fled the scene with my basket; leaving behind me the distressed cries of young Master Speirs, a very pale and cadaverous youth some ten years of age, the fruit of a late passion of Mr. Speirs, at this time absent in Glasgow. Master Speirs doubtless imagined himself to have become an orphan by a fatal stroke; his echoing cries pursued me down the tenement stair and into the close; and hastened my footsteps.

Not far from this spot stands the trading-post of Mr. Campbell, fisherman and fish-monger.[31] His shop

---

31. A descendant of Mr. Campbell still owns this shop, and runs it much as his ancestor did. He is a resourceful and respectable man

is easy to find, since the stench of fish cuts around several corners, way-laying the foot-passenger, and creeping
like acrid smoke through every open window and door,
stinging the eye. Furthermore, Mr. Campbell suffers
from an affliction of the nose, brought on perhaps by the
consumption of fish and cheese in remarkable quantities,
which causes him to snort wetly like a pig and expel im-
pressive quantities of mucus upon the floor of his shop.
It is the case that many residents of the town of Dundee
owe Mr. Campbell money. I am in that unhappy position; but I wondered if there might be a way in which I
could dispose of the foot and also cancel my debts, by
one swift blow. If Mr. Campbell could be persuaded to
exchange my debts for this remarkable foot, my morning's work would not be in vain. Hastening to his shop, I
found the fisherman in gloomy contemplation of a lobster
whose age was uncertain, but which gazed back at Mr.
Campbell in sad anticipation of an unlucky day; perhaps
Mr. Campbell was pondering whether it might still find
a sale among the poorest of the town, were he to drop the
price by another bodle or so; I managed to attract his –
that is, Mr. Campbell's – attention briefly, and we retired
behind a filthy blood-stained curtain of sailcloth, by which
furnishing of modesty he spared his customers the worst
visions of his preparatory activities.

---

from whom fresh fish of the highest quality are, without fail, to be
purchased. We have the strongest admiration for any man who sets
forth upon the seas, for there can be no more perilous trade. We
recommend his shop to all of our Readers. On production of this
volume, Mr. Campbell undertakes to agree an advantageous price
with the customer for any item purchased.

"I have," I whispered to Mr. Campbell, in as loud a whisper as I dared, Mr. Campbell having gone deaf two years ago after a particularly fierce struggle with a cod at the mouth of the River Tay, "I have in my possession," I stated, "an item which, I am advised by Dr. Blair himself, has the most marvellous and most powerful properties of attraction to the fish of the sea."

"Eh?" asked Mr. Campbell blankly, casting another eye distractedly over the lobster which he had been sure to carry with him.

"Bait," I explained, inwardly cursing my weakness for the long words and phrases that Dr. Blair uses. "I have the strongest bait here that you have ever laid eyes on."

On hearing that word, Mr. Campbell immediately came to life; he snorted and hawked enthusiastically. "Let me see it then!" he exclaimed and pulled back the piece of cloth which I had thought to drape over the Elephant's foot. He eyed it with scepticism. I thought it best to list all its undoubted attributes.

"The flesh of the Elephant," I lectured, as might Dr. Blair before an audience of gullible philosophers and burgesses, "is known throughout the Oriental world as being of the greatest attraction to both the wild beasts of the mountain and the mighty fishes of the sea. Indeed," I went on, seizing inspiration from the interested gaze of the lobster, "among the whalers of Portugal, the foot of the Elephant is prized as the very greatest bait. This is, as you will know, the foot of a Portuguese Elephant, bred especially for the whalers."

Mr. Campbell was easily persuaded. "The Good Lord preserve us!" he muttered, his eyes narrowing as he examined the drying flesh and yellow bones. "With this, I could catch such fish." He drifted off into a dream from which, as time flew past, I had to shake him. When I did so, the lobster waved an admonitory claw at me. "Such fish. Such fish," he repeated. Then his face grew wrathful. I feared it was because he had seen through my ruse; but it was only that the thought of his enemies upon the River Tay and other reaches of the high seas had soured his temper.

"Do you know," says he, shaking the lobster within an inch of its life, "that it is hard now to find a living upon the River? I row out each day to chase the salmon, and there they are, dozens of them, spoiling the fishing!"

"The salmon are spoiling the fishing?" I asked, unsure of his drift.

"No, sir," said he, "those tykes from Broughty Ferry and Newburgh and such places. Then," said he, warming to his theme, and expelling snotter from all possible openings, "you have the Dutchmen — pah! The Dutchmen — first they send us their king, then they come here in their big fancy boats and seize all the fish from under the seas, as they have seized all the whales from the north. Scarce a herring or a flounder remains for me! I am reduced to this!" He shook the lobster under my nose. "This sort of creature is all I am left with! I cannot sell this — I might as well throw it back into the sea!" The lobster knew not whether to be insulted or relieved, but winked encouragingly at Mr. Campbell. His wrath died a bit and a light shone in his eyes. "You say the men of Portugal prize this for the whale? Then perhaps I might turn a profit with the men of Holland. Have you seen how they catch the whale?" I admitted that I had not been upon the sea at all, let alone seen a whale being trapped. Mr. Campbell nodded patronisingly at my land-bound lack of experience.

"Aye well," he continued, "when a man such as myself goes out to catch the herring or the haddock or the whiting or the cod, he takes with him a good firm line and as many hooks as his family can bait in a day – perhaps three or four hundred hooks to the line. Then it is just a question of dropping the line where he judges it best. When I was younger, I could come home with every hook taken, and a boat full of fish – those were days, Mr. Orum, those were days!"[32] He stroked the lobster tenderly as he remembered the far-off triumphs of his youth, and I feared that I would spend much of the morning in his company. But he soon returned to his matter. "So, when it comes to catching the whale, I am advised that the line is a good stout rope, such as you might hang a man with, and hooks made of iron, and bait the size of – well, Mr. Orum – bait the size of an Elephant's foot!"

Having brought himself to such a pitch of excitement, with attendant snorts, Mr. Campbell asked if he might purchase the foot. We negotiated terms of exchange, which we held to be to our mutual benefit: for my part of the bargain, all my past debts were forthwith annulled; for his part, he gained foot and basket and the fair promise of a profit with the despised Dutchmen when next they entered the harbour of Dundee. However, Mr. Campbell had not risen to such a height of mercantile prominence as he now occupied without a good dose of cunning.

---

32. Those days will, we are assured, return again, for the seas abound with herring and cod. As there can be no doubt that the Elephant and the Tiger will continue to walk the world, so we may rest easy that the shoals of fishes will never cease to move in their millions.

"Now then," said he, having first secured the lobster under his left arm, in order to shake on the deal with his right hand. The lobster realized at that moment that all hope was lost, and ceased to agitate its limbs. "Now then, would you have more of such −" he nodded at the left fore-foot "− such bait? That we might perhaps come to some arrangement?"

I asked him what he had in mind, but he refused to be drawn. Finally, I conceded that I did not at that moment have other items, but that I was in a position where I might be able to secure them for him. He was not, how-ever, a man to be held off by vague promises: without the benefits of any philosophical preparation, I had to list the various parts of the Elephant which I thought might prove attractive to the fish: the liver, the kidneys, the eyes especially prized by the seal-hunters of the far north − I promised Mr. Campbell that I would endeavour to bring him some or all of them. In so doing I felt that I had signed a pact with the Fisher after Lost Souls and that I was now ravelled in the Net of Perdition.[33] We shook hands again; the lobster ended its days among the living; and I made my way in haste to the house of Dr. Blair, trailing behind me such a stench of fish that half the cats of Dundee pad-ded after me, to the greater excitement of all the dogs of Dundee.

It was considerably later than nine o'clock by the time I reached Dr. Blair's house. By good fortune, the surgeon had been called away on a visit to some unfortunate soul

---

33. We feel that no commentary is necessary here: here is a man *claiming* to save the Last Elephant from Oblivion − but how does he act? He trades it piece by piece for his own life's necessities!

living out at Hawkhill, and was not expected back for an hour or so. The cook voiced her opinion of my piscine scent in a pithy phrase, and turned me out of her kitchen. I expressed surprise that she could smell anything at all over the stench of her cooking, being rewarded for my spirited opinion with her view that I "stank waur than a ****". I understood now just why so many of the cook's suitors had found solace in the forgetful bosom of the sea. Retiring to a safe distance for the sake of propriety, I washed myself down under the pump which stood in the back yard, and awaited the surgeon's return.

The Last Elephant stood beside me, warming her huge body in the Spring sunshine. "Gilbert Orum," said she solemnly, "you must cease to be the servant of Blair, the Master of Dissection. That man would reduce me stroke by stroke, cut by cut, to dust; I will end up as no more than words upon a page. Free yourself from him. You must build me up stroke by stroke, line by line, that your children may see me for what I AM, for all time. This is your duty, Gilbert."

I considered her commandment, but did not know how to reply. She reviewed one by one the tools of my trade, which she turned gently with her trunk: "Be the man you are, the skilled engraver, the equal of Dr. Blair. You should and must use your own skills to defeat the Butchers of the Earth."

It was a simple thing to decide, on these words, that Dr. Blair's path and mine should go separate ways. He wishes to preserve the Last Elephant by utterly destroying it, by sawing it into smaller pieces with his ever-meticulous examinations, until, at the end, all that would remain of her would be an Osteology. I, for my part, wish

to preserve the animal whole, depict it as it lived. To that
end will I work. He and I cannot agree – my obligation
to him should be at an end. To be sure: he needs me for
my engraving skills; and I need him for the remains of
the Elephant; but there is nothing, nothing at all, beyond
these ties of mutual necessity.

I paced up and down in some agitation, anxious to
engage. As I did so, I met Mrs. Blair, and young John
Blair, a lad of some three years of age, who emerged from
the house on some domestic errand. Mrs. Blair was heavy
with child. I stood and removed my hat, to offer her a
respectful greeting; young John scampered around with
a small dog; I pitied the young lad, for without doubt his
own father had designs upon that dog which were not
compatible with carefree scampering; Mrs. Blair returned
my greeting, asked after my family, which was very kindly
meant; and then took child and dog off down the lane.[34]

At length, Dr. Blair arrived in haste from whatever surgical matter he had attended, greeted me curtly, entered
the kitchen, stripped off his coat; and continued, as if no
delay had occurred, to wield knife and tongs upon the
pieces of the poor Elephant. I – he had no suspicion that

---

34. We are reliably informed by Mr. W.B. of Boston that Mrs.
Blair later produced, in strict order, Henry, Elizabeth, and Isabell
as brother and sisters to young John. In the year 1711, the family
moved from Dundee to our neighbouring town of Coupar Angus.
What became of the poor lady and her children when the Doctor
embarked in 1715 on his ill-advised adventure with the supporters
of the eighth King James, we do not know: we believe that Dr. Blair
left Coupar Angus in great haste for to invade England, his family
remaining safely behind. Perhaps one of our Readers can illuminate
the later family life of the Blairs?

I was no longer his unquestioning secretary – drew and scribbled and inhaled the stench of the carnage, while, in the background, the cook poured her many opinions into the red ears of the kitchen-maid who received the unwelcome intelligence by throwing herself into a wild spin.

Dr. Blair, clearly having continued his voracious study of works on Elephants, lectured relentlessly to Mr. Menteith, myself, Miss Gloag and the unfortunate maid on "the Manner of *Taking* them"; which manner is illustrative of the cunning, deceitful and treacherous nature of men, involving trickery and the untroubled exploitation of the Elephant's natural sympathies and desires. Worse was to follow in "the Manner of *Taming* them", in which amusement men employ sticks, ropes and the setting of one Elephant against another.

All of which seems to be proof of the cruelty inflicted by Man upon his fellow-creatures on land, sea and air. Take my own Elephant here, now lying in ever smaller pieces in the kitchen of the eminent Surgeon of Dundee, my *Florentia*: stolen from her mother; hauled from the wild forests and hills in which she roamed free; forced to perform sundry tricks and masquerades before cruel and intoxicated audiences; finally led by ropes across northern plains and stormy seas, far into the wilds of a boggy land; until, from exhaustion or fever, or from the unsavoury vapours of Broughty Ferry, she lay down and died. How many other animals, of similar docile nature, have been taken from their homes and left to die? How many other creatures, birds and fish have been taken from their natural world, not even for food, but simply for the sport and amusement of men? As many a man treats his fellow-man, so Man treats his fellow-creatures.[35]

Dr. Blair, in his warm kitchen, made a thorough examination of the amount of Fat contained within the body
of his victim, and expressed great surprise as he did so at
the leanness of the beast, finding little enough of "adipose
substance" in the places where he would expect to find it.
He passed harsh judgement on Mr. Santos, for his cruelty at having run the Beast so thin. Such a judgement I
considered not to be even-handed; but when I remarked
on the likelihood that the beast had dwindled as a result
of being taken from its home of a thousand hills, and the
easterly winds of Scotland had finally worn away all of its
fat; then Dr. Blair persuaded me that it was the duty of
Mr. Santos to have seen the animal well-fed and well-rest-
ed. I reflected on this, and began to consider Mr. Santos
and Giovanni in a new light, thinking that they might
have placed their own profit before the prosperity of the
Elephant. I openly deplored the sufferings of the poor
beast; but scarcely had I opened my mouth to express
an opinion that Dr. Blair interrupted me and delivered a
tedious lecture on the Great Philosophical Enterprise in
which he was engaged.

"Mr. Orum," said he severely, as he had told me
many times before, "it is not for me to question the ways
in which the bounty of the Wise Governor falls in my
road, but rather to take up that bounty and to examine it

35. Men are surely put on Earth to have *Dominion* over Animals?
Or have we been misled? A gentleman must have concerns for the
well-being of his wife, his horse, his cattle, his dog; a gentleman
need have no concern for the Wild Brutes of the Earth, from whose
skins he may make coats. Mr. Orum's concerns are not worthy of a
civilized Briton.

thoroughly, that I may thereby understand and appreciate the wonders of Creation. If thereby," he continued, wagging a large knife at various unnamed parts of the beast, "if thereby I hit upon an understanding of the causes of fevers and death in my fellow-man, then I should not hesitate to take up this understanding, and pass it on to others, that the health of the nation of Scotland may be improved. This is a Great Principle."

I had no argument to venture on this matter: I am no Philosopher; I will not engage in battle with Dr. Blair's chosen weapons, only with my own. If, in this new Eighteenth Century, Man is to lay bare all the clock-work and machinery of Nature; then I am not one to stand as an obstacle. I wish only to state here that I have the gravest of doubts about the wisdom and benefits of delving so deeply into the secrets of Creation. Dr. Blair's vision that Philosophers will discover and label all things upon land, in the air and under the sea – which great task he imagines will easily be complete by the end of his own life – this may reveal matters which are neither palatable to the people of Dundee, nor profitable to Man.

I was not rationed to this one lecture, for Dr. Blair insisted on telling us of other Elephants which had come to Scotland, or places beyond their natural range; among which were an Elephant which toured Scotland some twenty years previous to our beast (but – possibly to its good fortune – did not come to Dundee). Dr. Blair found great significance in the fact that this earlier Elephant arrived at around the time when William of Orange was installed as King of Britain, in direct opposition to what was right and proper for the thrones of both Scotland and England; and that our Elephant arrived in Great Britain

at around the time when a further great injustice was being perpetrated upon the people of Scotland, with "this
Treaty of Union". From his argument, it became evident
that an Elephant arrived in Scotland each time some
catastrophe befell its people. Whether he is right in this
matter, or no, I cannot tell, having very little of the political learning of Dr. Blair.[36]

However, he was soon diverted into a narration of other Elephants examined by Philosophers of an earlier age.
In Dublin, some years ago, there was a male Elephant
which was unfortunately burned to death when the stable
in which it was housed caught fire. Are all beasts brought
into captivity destined to die in an unnatural way?[37]

---

36. Dr. Blair had, by an extraordinary leap of insight, hit upon
a co-incidence which the present Editor has noted earlier in this
volume. Our surgeon's political views on the Act of Union may be
forgiven, since many a man of that time looked with some degree of
trepidation upon a Union with England – a Union which has since
brought us so many benefits! We are now a proud island race, we
Britons.

37. Dr. Moulins of Dublin was able to dissect some of the
uncharred parts of that beast and make notes of an anatomical
nature; Dr. Blair confirmed that Dr. Moulins prepared many
notes on the *Penis* and *Testes* of that creature. Dr. Moulins – said
he – made but an inconclusive account of the dissection, partly
because of the crisped state of the cadaver, partly because the Irish
butchers were as the butchers of Dundee of that time – energetic
with their knives, unskilled with their hands. "It was no fault of his
that Dr. Moulins made an imperfect examination," writes Dr. Blair
charitably, "for the animal seems, while burning to death, to have
wrestled and struggled tremendously, and been much torn and
charred in the engulfing flames."

It was late in the afternoon before Dr. Blair consented to release me from my labours. I made haste to the shop of Mr. Campbell, to follow up our recent bargain, for I thought that my poor family should at least take some profit from the accidents of the day. Mr. Campbell was pleased to furnish me with some fish that he had caught "only last week"; and then, as I was hastening from the shop, advised me that he had already disposed of the left fore-foot of the deceased Elephant. I was surprised by this news, since I did not imagine the Dutchmen would have been in harbour quite so soon.

"No," said Mr. Campbell, "I found a customer far closer to home than those perfidious Dutch."

"Oh," said I, wondering which other fishermen of the town he might have wished to dupe, or, indeed, put in direct competition with himself for the largest fishes of the deep.

"Indeed," said Mr. Campbell, "I have sold it to Mr. Blair."

It is no great exaggeration to state that my heart sank within me, as a stone within a well. If he had passed in on to Dr. Blair, then surely Dr. Blair would have asked for, and been given the name of, the previous owner. I was surely lost!

Seeing my confusion, the fish-monger snorted and spat snotter on the floor in what I understood to be an act of deepest amusement. "Ah, Mr. Orum, not your Dr. Blair, but his cousin, Mr. Alexander Blair."

While I supported myself against Mr. Campbell's door-jamb, and let relief fill my soul once more, the man told me that Mr. Alexander Blair, Provost of this town, and the patron of a Party dedicated to ensuring that Mr. George Yeaman did not succeed to that civic honour; had sent his cook down from his residence on Balgayhill to purchase some turbot. Mr. Campbell and the cook being old friends, the matter of the Elephant's fore-foot had been idly discussed. Upon the cook's return to Balgayhill, her master had caught wind of the foot, and of its provenance; and had hastened down to discover more for himself. The final and end result being, that Mr. Alexander Blair had made a good offer to Mr. Campbell; Mr. Campbell had had no hesitation in accepting it; and the foot was now firmly established in Mr. Blair's house at the top of the hill. With this news I was dismissed, as Mr. Campbell wished to shut up shop and prepare for the night, to launch his boat upon the Face of the Deep and to hunt the beasts below.

What was I to do? While the foot remained in the possession of Mr. Blair, there was a strong possibility that Dr. Blair would come to hear of it; should he come to hear of it, it was almost certain that the evidence of my deceit would come to light, and I would lose my most profitable patron. While my wife cooked the fish for our supper, and while my mother howled in anticipation of such a treat, I turned over in my mind these oppressive thoughts.

Having decided on my best course of action, I left my family to their anxious concerns, and hurried out into the dusk to pay a visit upon Mr. Alexander Blair, for whom, in the past, I have undertaken a number of commissions of the pictorial art. Mr. Blair had stated himself to be particularly pleased by an engraving of his handsome house, and it was with appropriate words reminding me of his pleasure that he received me in his business-room. Not knowing how best to approach the matter, I went at it head-on.

"Sir," I said as boldly as I could manage, "I believe you have in your possession an item of anatomical nature which properly belongs to another."

In reply, Mr. Blair merely raised his eye-brows. This hardly encouraged me to continue; but, keeping my eyes upon my engraving of his house, which hung above a roaring fire, I advanced my argument, explaining that the item had come into my possession and that I had in-tended to return it to Dr. Patrick Blair forthwith; that Mr. Campbell had persuaded me – by what means I did not reveal: but gave out that it was against my better judge-ment – to sell it to him; that I now repented of this rash contract, and wished to bring the item back into my pos-session and make peace with my conscience.

Mr. Blair then responded, without actually naming the Elephant's foot by its proper name, but referring to it in oblique manner as "the item in question", by stating that he had paid Mr. Campbell good money for it, and that he had no intention of relinquishing it to his cousin Patrick. "Has Dr. Blair," he asked me, "not three other items of like nature to play his games with?" I conceded that that might be the case. "Well, then," said Mr. Blair, "leave me with my one item to play my own games. Do not worry, Mr. Orum," he added, seeing my despair, "I shall not divulge how the item in question came into my possession. In recognition of your past service to my fam-ily, your secret is safe with me.

Not inclining to take his assertions and assurances at face-value,[38] I asked Mr. Blair what he intended with "the item in question".

He led me to understand that this was not my concern. However, he made clear his belief that God would not have put an Elephant in the way of the contenders for office in Dundee, had He not expected some advantage to arise from it. "Yeaman has at present the advantage," he said, "but it is certain that the item in question will determine the outcome of the coming Election for Provost."

With that, he ushered me from his house, and I stumbled down the path to the town, to return to my family. I sit now, sleepless again, in confused speculation on the enigmatical nature of the left fore-foot of the Last Elephant and its possible influence upon the Town Council.[39] I seem embarked on a long dream with no happy outcome.

---

38. An extraordinary impertinence from one whose every utterance is a Libel and a Lie!

39. Mr. Orum seems non-plussed by our well-ordered System of Government. Without men of character, like Mr. Alexander Blair, acting for the *Greater Good*, and constrained by the well-managed levers of *Democracy*, would not our towns, our cities, our very country fall into *Revolution*, *Chaos* and untrammelled *Disrepair*, as we have seen in France and America, and – more recently – Brazil?

2 MAY 1706.

For the first time in five days, I was last night able to sleep for several hours; it was not restful; my dreams were filled with blood, gore, and the last words of the Ultimate Elephant. I shouted out and woke my wife and children. My mother, we must thank Providence, was not in the slightest bit disturbed.

On this, the second, day of May in the year 1706, Dr. Blair and I worked from dawn until dusk at the dissection, identification and classification of the remaining inner parts of the Elephant. For all our efforts, Dr. Blair described our task as a 'superficial description'; he, perhaps, found the results unsatisfactory; for my part, I know not what better we could have done.

We attacked the *Proboscis*, or Nose; the Liver, Spleen and Kidneys; and the Heart. The cook cursed at the prospect of being displaced yet again from her realm.

"Dr. Blair," said she forbiddingly, "I will away to my sister up at Fintry if I can not have my kitchen back. This is a ******* outrage upon my person!"

Her employer calmed her with an onslaught of words, the drift whereof was that she would be proud, in later years, to look back on these days and tell her nephew that she had been witness to the greatest dissection of an Elephant that had ever taken place in Scotland. At the mere mention of her nephew, Miss Gloag's mouth contracted and she sobbed into a large cloth. Dr. Blair put his arms round her broad shoulders, then dispatched her upstairs; and we set to.

Plunging about with a knife in the midst of the

Elephant's head, directed by Dr. Blair to make this cut
or that cut, to slice here "carefully!"; or to saw there
"without tearing!"; I could not take the broader view of
what it was we struggled with. At brief interludes I was
permitted, after washing my hands in a bucket of warm
water, to put down the butcher's knife and pick up the
more familiar tools of my own craft and trade.

What astonishes me more than anything in Dr. Blair's
method is that he is able to study the muscles of the dead
animal – no, not even the dead animal, merely dissected
and butchered parts thereof – and imagine the whole as
a live animal, gaily exhibiting to us all its many skills and
tricks with the famed trunk.[40] To my knowledge, he had
never seen *Florentia* when she still stepped among the living. He can bring the beast to life before our very eyes;
and yet he chooses to destroy it, piece by piece.

---

40. We will take the opportunity here to refer to Dr. Blair's
lucid – nay, poetical – indeed, exquisite – description of that day's
investigations on the 27th page of his famous Essay, where he
describes the muscles comprizing the *Erectores Proboscidis* and the
Retractores Proboscidis:

"Thus you see a wonderful Contexture of 4 Muscles, so contriv'd
as to perform all kinds of Motions; for as either in the Femora or
Humerus, from Erection, Extention, Adduction and Abduction,
proceeds a circular Motion; so here when the Elevator and
Depressor, or Retractor act together on either side, then there is a
lateral Motion: And when the Congener Elevatores and Retractores
act, then there is either Elevation or Depression; and from these
two, with lateral Motions on both Sides successively perform'd,
proceeds a circular Motion. But this is not all; we see that any part of
the Trunk, either Root or Extremity, or both at once, can be bended
either upwards or downwards."

Our investigations of the *Proboscis* took up a large part
of the morning, and I was glad to be able to sit down to
a dinner left out for me in the yard; where again I was
closely observed by the huge black cat and the spinning
kitchen-servant; again to their deepest disappointment.
After barely half-an-hour, we turned without further
respite to the investigation of the Liver, the *Glandulae
Renales* and the Kidneys, in such detail that I almost immediately regretted having re-filled my stomach. Dr. Blair
was, however, in good humour, for he proceeded without
any caution to quadrate, or compare, the internal organs
of the Elephant to those Commissioners who, as we
hacked and cut, were "cutting and butchering the Body
Politick of Scotland".[41]

"And who shall we say, Mr. Orum," he asked me,
brandishing a surgeon's saw at me from the other side of
the main portion of the Elephant's cadaver, "who is the
Proboscis amongst those Commissioners who seek to sell
Scotland to the English Parliament?"

With all the politeness which I could muster in the
face of this blustering nonsense, I begged ignorance, not
being well acquainted with the matters of Government,
still less with the names of those appointed by the Queen
to arrange our affairs.

"But, Gilbert," remonstrated my patron, in mocking

---

41. In the passage which follows, Dr. Blair takes an almost
unpardonable liberty with the reputations of the leading figures of
Scotland in those days. For all that some carping was made by men
such as George Lockhart of Carnwath, or Mr. Fletcher of Saltoun,
it is quite clear that scarcely any man profited personally from the
Union; or acted in any way ignobly.

tones, "you must not let yourself remain in ignorance! Whose destiny is it that they are deciding in Edinburgh and London, if not yours and mine? Should we not," he demanded, indicating as he did so some new cut to be made by Mr. Menteith, "at least discover what they are up to?"

I made some form of answer, which he ignored; he continued: "They have barely begun to meet and to dis-sect the body of Scotland. But let me suppose that the *Proboscis* among them all is the Duke of Argyll, eh? Or maybe Lord Dundas – aye, let it be Dundas, sniffing and twirling, circling this way and that, as all his muscles el-evatory and retractory guide him. Dundas would be the thing!"

Dr. Blair was greatly amused and contented with his own witticism; and this kept him quiet for a while, as we set in upon the Liver. This organ was beyond the ordinary size of a liver, being 36 inches long and 22 inches at the broadest part. The surgeon was most pleased with this organ, as it seems it was one of the few which his battalion of butchers and fellow-physicians had managed to extract in a single piece from the corpse; he was also inordinately satisfied to find that, in structure, substance and texture, it was in no way different from the livers extracted from other animals.

"A liver is a liver, Mr. Menteith," he assured his man-servant, who obsequiously expressed an interest in the matter. "It has one function among all of God's creatures, so let us be not astonished to find its form to be identical with all others." Alas, at this moment, he was reminded of his earlier amusement, and informed us that the liver, "being the same regardless of which body you put it into,

must be the Earl of Mar."[42] This notion he found so diverting that he was obliged to go in search of his wife and
share it with her; while he did so, Mr. Menteith and I
continued to beat our way through the guts.

Dr. Blair much regretted that the Gall and the
Pancreas had been taken away by the butchers, for, he
said, "discerning men are *excited* to find out the uses of
the Galls of different animals." The Spleen, which was
three and one-half feet long, I spent some considerable
time in sawing at, with very little *excitement*; and then in
copying, with far greater *satisfaction*.

The Spleen appears to have been something of a disappointment to him, although quite what his surgical intentions were, I am not certain. He spent some time in blowing it up with a small pair of bellows, filched from Miss
Gloag when her back was turned, and then in pressing
out of it some 'venal grumous blood'. I cannot describe
the feelings of horror which I experienced in witnessing
the surgeon's 'pressing' of the blood. It was a sight from
which I had to run precipitately into the yard, to gulp
down the fresh air of Dundee; some minutes elapsed before I ventured inside again, to face the insolent thrusts of
Mr. Menteith, and the ironical concern of Dr. Blair, who
had started in on the Kidneys; on which we need spend
little time; for Dr. Blair in the end grew impatient, as the

---

42. Once more, we must be lenient with the political views of men
of Bygone Times, who did not have the longer view of History; the
House of Mar is a great one, and it is certain that conspiring tongues
have unjustly maligned it. Mr. Orum may perhaps have mis-heard
– or mis-represented, for he is by no means trustworthy – the views
of Dr. Blair.

afternoon was already drawing to a close; and the main
course and entertainment of the day, for all of us, was the
Elephant's Heart.

Whether the Heart be the residence of the Soul, or of
Love, or of God, or of Religion or Morality, I do not claim
to have any knowledge; what is certain is that, without the
Heart, a creature does not live. Therefore I felt keenly the
dissection of that organ, since, once dissected, it could
not be restored; once the Heart is removed, *Death Enters
In*. It was evident that Dr. Blair was not in any way as'
tonished by the heart, for he was almost careless in his
reply when I asked to make a drawing of it. Disregarding
his lack of interest, I took my time, feeling that it was my
duty and responsibility to honour the great beast's heart,
even if our surgeon did not. I am perhaps the only man to
have drawn such an organ, and no man will do so after me.
Within the next few days, that heart will no longer exist.

What did interest Dr. Blair, however, was something
he found within the chambers of the heart. This was a
fatty white substance, much like lace or seaweed, which
he named the *Polypus*, and which he was pleased to spread
out across the floor of the kitchen and examined with an
eye'glass. We were forbidden to step upon it; at which
command, the kitchen'maid nervously launched herself
upon her twirling and had to be ejected with consider'
able force into the yard, where she continued blinking and
spinning in the lowering sun.

"Mr. Orum", said my patron, "step over here and
sketch this for me." I carried out my duty as he ordered,
and drew with absolute exactitude the curious growth
which he had extracted from within the heart. The cook,
for the moment imprisoned in a corner of her kitchen,

was fascinated by it. "Is that the soul of the Elephant?" she asked, for once employing neither crude words nor curses, such was her awe. Dr. Blair pondered; and then declared that he did not know; but that he thought that it was not.

"The *Polypus*," he said, displaying his extensive learn-ing, "is named after the Greek word meaning 'many-footed'. As I can see if I look closely, this has many feet or branches. But what is a wonder is that it has crept in to every corner of the heart, and, holding so much fat, is likely to kill the beast."

I was about to interrupt – the animal was already dead – but I thought better of it. Dr. Blair was, after all, my employer for this week at least.

"And so," he mused, reverting to his game of compar-ing the Elephant to the distant Commission sitting to debate the Treaty of Union; "And so it will be like the body of their Great-Britain, which is proposed; at its heart, so many crawling after their own profit, so many collecting the fat that, at last, the Union will die on its feet." He gazed around him soberly. "What do we think, Mr. Orum?" he asked.

I said that I knew not, only that the Elephant was al-ready dead, so perhaps it was this *Polypus* which killed it? Dr. Blair shook his head impatiently, and turned away. So I cannot present any of his philosophical knowledge on this matter; but it does seem to me that, while Dr. Blair conjectured that the *Polypus* might yet kill the beast, it had, as far as I could tell, already died; and that suddenly.[43]

Night had long since fallen, and the many candles were dripping their hot wax upon our weary hands, when

Dr. Blair announced that we might cease our labours. "But be sure to attend early tomorrow, for another day of Philosophy awaits!" Aye, thought I, another sinful day of destruction awaits.

---

43. Once more, we are obliged to refer to Dr. Blair's Essay to make sense of Mr. Orum's obscure gabbling:

"The Auricles were large, and the Left as well as the Right full of grumous Blood. At the opening of the Ventricles, I found them both fill'd with the same Polypus; which strangely twisted itself in among the Valves [...] and also among the fleshy Columns at the bottom of each Ventricle [...] These Polypus's, from a massy Substance in the middle of the Ventricle, sent forth to all Parts their Branches, which here and there twisted themselves round these fleshy Columns, their tendinous Insertions, and the tendinous Fibres of the Valves, with a wonderful Intricacy. In a word, there was no Angle, no Corner or Cavity, which the Polypus did not occupy: And yet so much was it disengag'd from the Substance of the Heart, and 'twas so strong and tough, that by pulling its grosser part in the middle, all the other Branches mov'd; and by cutting a few Parts of it, where it was most engag'd, and where the fleshy Columns were thickest, I got it out altogether; and having stretch'd it out, did pleasantly behold these Ramifications, proceeding from its grosser part like so many Thongs or Laces whereinto a piece of Leather had been cut, some broad and some narrower; but none very thick; of a yellow Colour, and fat substance; each of them weighing 1 lb. which I may safely say was more Fat than was upon all the Body beside. From whence I may reasonably conclude, that altho' it had not met with the formerly mention'd Hardships, however it might have liv'd sometime, yet it could not live long, it being evident, that this Polypus would at length have prov'd its Ruin."

3 MAY 1706.

Last night, I sat long writing in my Journal, speculating on
the Philosophy of Dr. Blair and failing again to sleep for
more than two hours: I was awake well before the sun, I
lay worrying for – it seemed – many more hours, then rose
quietly to embark on an errand. I stopped by the shop of
Mr. Seton, the butcher.[44] I intended to clear my debts with
a number of the tradesmen of Dundee, in the same way as
I had dealt with Mr. Campbell, the fish-monger.

Mr. Seton was not greatly pleased to see me in his
shop, and undertook to serve every one else who entered
before he turned to me.

"Mr. Orum," he stated, without that smile of invitation which he reserved for everyone else in Dundee.

I hesitated; but then took courage from the fact that
the shop was, apart from ourselves and a fat boy dabbling
in tripe, empty.

"Mr. Seton," said I, "I have here –" at which I patted a canvas sack with which I had left Dr. Blair's house
the previous evening, under cover of the darkness, "– the
largest kidneys you have ever beheld."

I had, it seemed, uttered some magical word, for Mr.
Seton's attitude changed immediately. "Kidneys, eh?" he
murmured, cleaning his bloody hands on a filthy cloth in
eager anticipation. "Well, I'm always keen for kidneys;
let me see them!"

---

44. We can find no trace of Mr. Seton or his descendants in
Dundee. But we must, unwillingly, suppose that Mr. Orum has not
conjured the man from his fantasies.

I deposited on his slab some of the contents of my sack. Mr. Seton gasped and put both hands to his mouth in unconcealed delight. The two kidneys were astonishingly large. Indeed, as we had measured on the previous day, the two kidneys were each one foot in length and six inches in breadth. But, against all denial, kidneys.[45]

Mr. Seton was struck dumb. The boy, sensing some wonder from the sudden silence of his guide through life, suspended his dealings with the tripe, and approached. He, being his father's son and appreciative of all matters in butchery, could not prevent his eyes from bulging in their sockets; his ruddy face shone brightly with sweat; he squeaked in excitement.

"Mr. Orum," gasped Mr. Seton at last.

"Mr. Seton," said I, waiting for his offer.

"Such kidneys," sighed the butcher, evidently content to stand there all day, held in thrall by a sight that few butchers before him had seen, and none – though he knew it not – would ever see again.

Impatient as I was to see an end to the business and take up my duties at the house of Dr. Blair, I asked him what he might pay for them. At last, after persistent questioning, and my move to put the items back in the sack, he was persuaded to strike a deal – in spirit and general content, much like the one concluded with Mr. Campbell earlier in the week: to wit, the annulment of all debts, and a certain amount of credit to be stored up against future purchases. We shook hands on it.

---

45. Mrs. S. frequently told us that a well-cooked kidney was better for a man's happiness than a compliant woman. We bowed to her judgement; but remarked inwardly that that was not always the case during our younger years.

Uplifted by my success, I passed quickly to the shop of Mr. Campbell, and bartered with him such a portion of the Spleen as I had been able to retrieve: I passed it off as excellent for catching mackerel. He was much pleased with our new arrangements; and I was able to return home with six smoked herring, which my family greatly enjoyed for breakfast; although my wife enquired whether "These did not come from Hendrie?" I assured her that my brother had not been involved, and that we might enjoy our kippers with a clear conscience.[46] We did so.

I hastened then to the house of Dr. Blair, and we set to on our second day of the Anatomical Description of the Elephant's Parts. This day, announced the surgeon, he would dissect and describe the Mouth and Tongue, the Brain, and the *Partes Generationi Inservientes*; "Otherwise known," he whispered loudly to Miss Gloag, "as the organs of matrimony!" Miss Gloag, to her very great credit, blushed, retreated outside to the yard and terrorized the maid. James Menteith, coarse and dark wee creature that he is, laughed fit to burst; and took every opportunity for the rest of the day to introduce into the conversation the words *Generation Party*; and applaud his own great wit. Never have I felt so alone at my work as today!

However, scarcely had we begun our task, than there was an interruption caused by Miss Gloag's ushering in of Mr. Robertson. Our minister is a man of around three-score years, with one good eye; he is as thin as a pole, unexpectedly strong and never known to be lost for words – commonly those which righteously condemned the ways of the world. Dr. Blair makes no secret of his

---

46. A conscience, without doubt, easily salved!

view that Mr. Robertson is an Enemy of Philosophy; today he welcomed the man of God caustically.

"Ah!" said he, straightening his wig, "The last remaining representative of the United Original Secession
Church!" This is a weary and long-standing witticism
of his, referring to an earlier episode in Mr. Robertson's
life and work; a witticism which Mr. Robertson rightly
ignores. "Have you come to see my Elephant?" he continued, gesturing cheerily towards the slowly diminishing pile of flesh and gore as he did so. "I am studying the
organs of reproduction of the Elephant. You will no doubt
recognize these?"

"I have not and I do not," said Mr. Robertson, in response to the two impertinent questions, his mighty voice
filling the kitchen. "For the ways of an Elephant are alone
the ways of God. As you should know, sir. It is the ways
of men under the Judgement of God Almighty alone that
interest me; as they should you, Dr. Blair."

"Why, yes, Mr. Robertson: the ways of men and of
God are precisely what interest me too. Indeed, it is this
Elephant now lying before us that reveals to us the ways
of God in their unanswerable magnificence. Would you
not agree?"

Mr. Robertson was quite unwilling to agree, arguing
long and powerfully that it was not for men to "poke their
noses into the glorious work and ways of the Almighty."
A crowd began to gather outside in the yard, for Mr.
Robertson's voice carries far and wide, and his opinions
are much-respected. Dr. Blair, for his part, and with no
sign of shame or fear, argued from quite the opposed
stance: "If Man, who is, you will agree, the most perfect
of all creatures –"

Mr. Robertson rightly interrupted: "Man, of all the creatures of God, is far from being the most perfect, Dr. Blair, as you must know in your own heart!"

Dr. Blair ignored him: "– if Man does not, as you describe it, poke his nose in to the great wonders of the bodies of men and of animals, how is he to understand the supreme power of the Lord?"

"We can understand it, Dr. Blair," said Mr. Robertson coldly, "from the works of God as they appear to us, from the miracles told in the Bible, from the martyrdom of the saints of Scotland, not –" he looked around at the dis-membered Elephant, "– not from guddling around in gore and offal, which is the work of idle hands, and the pastime of an obdurate and impenitent Sinner!" With these words of condemnation, Mr. Robertson abandoned the Charnel-house of Blair, and set out to reveal to them-selves further sinners, of which the town of Dundee has always an unending supply; although not every sinner was engaged, day in and day out, in slicing open the most miraculous works of God with a sharp knife. Dr. Blair, for his part, shook his head at the words of Mr. Robertson; made an obscure comment to Menteith; and returned to his labour of the moment.

Which was: the identification, firstly, of the Intimate Parts; secondly, of the Mouth and Tongue; thirdly, should day-light and the passing of the hours permit, of the Brain.

Mr. Menteith, on being advised that we were to re-turn to the *Generation Parties*, was greatly inspired; and set to with his knife, keenly attending to every command from the doctor. At these same words being spoken, Miss Gloag absented herself from the kitchen, announcing that this was no place for a lady; perhaps all three gentlemen present considered the same appropriate response; but not one of us dared to express it in words. The dissection of these intimate parts occupied us for some interesting minutes, during which Dr. Blair took the occasion of Miss Gloag's absence to seize again her bellows and inflate the *Uterus*, remarking after he had done so certain nodules which appeared on that organ. Both Mr. Menteith and I observed this with some trepidation, not knowing quite how the thing would go; or, indeed, whither. But there was no accident, and Dr. Blair was satisfied with such measurements as he made. He then undertook a detailed examination of items in close proximity to the *Uterus*, using fingers and a sharp knife, complaining that the "butchers have hacked this about!" I confess I felt ill at the sight, and was obliged to seek fresh air in the yard, and to wash my head with cold water from the pump.[47]

----

47. If, Mr. Orum, we could yet apostrophize you, we would confirm that you are indeed a man of weak constitution. We have only retained this passage in the man's Journal because it sheds light upon his character and therefore his reliability as a witness, and to contrast it with Dr. Blair's cool and enlightened interest in the Elephant's *reproductive* organs. Which are presented to the Reader with far more propriety:

"All agree," writes Dr. Blair, "that it is an Animal of extraordinary modesty, and therefore never copulates in view of any; which because 'tis a big unwieldy Body, hath put authors to a loss as to the Posture. Some asserting that it is Retrocoient and Retromingent; among whom is Dr. Moulins, from an Observation he has made of the Situation and Structure of the Penis."

It is clear from further paragraphs in Dr. Blair's work, which we have examined in the most minute detail, that he made an intimate

After a consideration of the Bladder, which could contain, in Dr. Blair's estimation, some six or seven English
gallons, a figure provoking Mr. Menteith's greatest admiration, and a comparison by my patron of this organ

---

study of the method of copulation of a number of different animals:
hares, cats, rabbits, dogs, and Man; although matters relating to the
last creature are couched in Latin, to protect the innocent reader.
We do not shirk our Editorial responsibilities, in citing one example
relating to the Elephant:

"Others observing the distance between the Anus and the
Vagina," writes Dr. Blair, "and that the Duggs are situated between
the fore Limbs, are of Opinion, that the Female is in a Supine, and
the Male in a Prone Posture: among whom is Tavernier.'"

But Dr. Blair did not share Mr. Tavernier's opinion of the
posture of the male and the female, preferring, after close analysis
of the articulation of the fore-legs and hind-legs, to imagine the
copulation of the Elephant to be similar to that of the dog. These
are fascinating matters, when presented under a strictly Scientific
or Philosophical light, and not half-hidden in Shadow, as Mr. Orum
has done.

When he came to set down a record of this part of his
Examination, Dr. Blair wrote in a most scientific manner, of which
we have no cause to complain, noting – after he had "strictly ty'd the
Vagina" to observe whether air passed out of the Uterus – that that
intimate female organ "was very small and narrow, not admitting
above two or three Fingers", but that he could not measure its
"precise length [...] because I know not how much of it might have
been cut off" by the butchers. That Mr. Orum, or any other person,
should feel unmanned by this transaction, or the description thereof,
suggests to us only the depth of his moral deficiency.

One word of Caution: we would urge most earnestly that the
passages above not be read out aloud to the Impressionable Young,
nor read at all on the Sabbath Day.

to the Duke of Queensberry;[48] I took my dinner, during which I kept my eye firmly upon certain redundant parts of the *Partes Generationi Inservientes*, thinking perhaps to make a trade with the candle-maker, who has a mind which tends freely to ungovernable intimacy; and then we gathered again around the head for the opening of the skull and examination of the Brain.

The Brain was a disappointment to Dr. Blair. He has handled many brains of the dead and dying, and must have considered that something which so fills the Head, wherein reside our most powerful senses of the Eyes, the Ears, the Nostrils and the Mouth, must be of some significance. But no – it was merely big and soft, and soon put to one side, on top of a growing pile of discarded organs, after I had been instructed to copy it faithfully from life into my notebook. He passed some witty remark on the Brain being like unto the Duke of Hamilton: "undoubt-edly important, but nevertheless dull, damp and some-what soft to the touch"; which comparison he repeated many times, with much laughter.[49]

---

48. We need not remind our readers that this comparison, if truly made by Dr. Blair – a supposition we find unlikely, since he makes no mention of it in his Essay – was made at a time of Great Political Passion. Nothing need be deduced from this idle remark, except perhaps Mr. Orum's love of Libel.

49. We will not pass comment, for none is needed, on this libellous assertion by Mr. Orum. Instead, let us turn our attention to Dr. Blair's concise description of the brain:

"Being come to the Head, I have very little remarkable to add in this Place: For the Brain itself very little differeth from that of an Human one, except in bigness, and somewhat in Figure; the other being somewhat Oval, and this more round. The Dura Mater

Having found but little meat for his philosophical experiments in the Brain, Dr. Blair was inclined to stop work for the day; and I was soon dismissed, while he returned, covered with blood, to the bosom of his family.

I stored my instruments and notebooks in a place of safety, cleaned myself as best I could at the pump, and looked around carefully: all witnesses, except the large black cat, had vanished from the yard. The pile of offal was left unguarded. I made my way cautiously toward it, ever with an eye upon the over-looking windows, and retrieved from the pile the things from which I thought I might gain profit. Unfortunately, someone had already made off with the Heart, thinking as I did that it would fetch a fair price amongst the traders of Dundee – in this matter, my suspicions alight on the mercenary Mr. Menteith. With haste, I bundled up both the Brain and the *Partes Generationi Inservientes*. These I was surprised to discover, for if James Menteith had indeed been robbing the midden, he would most likely have secured these organs for his own dishonourable purposes. Concealing the items in my canvas sack, I hastened from the spot and made my way into the town. [50]

---

was a strong thick Membrane, every where disengag'd from the Pia Mater; which together with all the Substance of the Brain, was much more tender, soft, and flaccid, than could have been expected. Whether this proceeded from keeping the Head 2 or 3 Days after the Animal dy'd, before it was dissected, the Weather being then very hot, or from the languid Distemper whereof it dy'd, I know not."

50. Here, we believe, we have reached the very nadir of Mr. Orum's activities: to steal so blatantly from his employer, to embezzle, to filch – and then to boast of it openly! Can any man justify such an action and hope to retain one tattered rag of credibility? We think not. So much for Mr. Orum.

I called first, as I had planned earlier in the day, upon the candle-merchant, Mr. Sutherland, a man from foreign parts: he was a native of Greenock, and thus most uncouth. As I made haste towards his shop, I calculated just how much to my advantage I had arranged my debts in the past few days – I had annulled those to the butcher and the fish-monger; now the chandler would follow; all that remained was the baker and one or two other tradesmen into whose clutches I had unfortunately and inadvertently fallen. Mr. Sutherland was behind his counter, glowering with some acrimony at several wooden chests which were piled up before him. The air was thick with the miasma of wax. I approached Mr. Sutherland, feeling slightly dizzy.

"What dae ye want?" he demanded. "I tellt ye last week – nae mair candles for ye, nae fours nor nae sixes neither, naething, not wan – no till ye pay up yer debts. Ye can suffer in the sinful darkness into which ye have plunged yerself, ye lazy *****!"

Containing my righteous anger at this cool welcome, I merely opened the sack under his nose and revealed its contents.

"What in G–d's name is that?" he wanted to know, flinching slightly at the salty, bitter scent which arose.

I lowered my voice and explained it as simply as I could, using words which would be familiar to him and not for recording with any precision in this memorial.

At a stroke, his whole demeanour changed.

"Guid G–d, it canna be true!" he muttered quietly to himself, flushing red across his face. His hands began to shake. "Are these thon pairts of a female Elephant which – ye ken – thon pairts?"

"Indeed they are," said I. "Taken this very day from Dr. Blair's house where – as you probably know – we have been dissecting the creature."

Mr. Sutherland breathed heavily and wiped sweat from his face. I feared he might work himself into an apoplexy, and that I would be obliged to call upon the surgeon's services; which would place me in an awkward situation, as far as explanations were concerned. I therefore closed the sack.

"How much dae ye want for them?" whispered Mr. Sutherland, furtively glancing up and down the close.

We soon arranged terms, and I left him. Barely had I taken two steps than I heard Mr. Sutherland slamming and bolting the door to his establishment, having decided to cease trading for the day; and turn his attentions to – who knows what? It was not for me to ask, nor for him to enlighten me. In my sack, I still had the Brain, and pondered where best to place this. Just at that moment, by an unhappy chance, my thoughts far distant from my feet, I turned a corner and – once more, as if my life revolved in a circle – ran straight into Miss Speirs, who screamed lightly before she realized who I was.

"Oh," said she in a fluster, "it is you, Gilbert." She arranged her hair and looked me up and down. "Have you come to apologize for your recent behaviour, then?"

Out of common courtesy, I now begged her forgiveness, using such words of self-abasement as I knew from long experience would make a mark with the lady. She was very easily persuaded and bowed her head in acknowledgement of my apology; and took the liberty of placing her arm in mine.

A man of my years can imagine other lives he might

have lived, had he once chosen differently; or if fate were to deal a sudden blow to his wife. Briefly, as I felt her arm in mine, and the curve of her bosom upon my elbow, and as a loose wisp of her hair blew across my cheek, I speculated.[51]

"And what," said she, flirting with me, "do you have in your wee bag, then? Is that the instruments of your trade?"

Doing my best to detach myself from her, I suggested that it was such.

"I do so admire your skills in the craft of engravure, Mr. Orum," said she, in a flighty manner. "Might I perhaps take a peep at all the funny little scrapers that you have?"

Before I could prevent her – for to do so would have obliged me to wrest her hands from the neck of the sack, and jostle with her in the broad day-light – she had opened the sack and poked her head almost all the way in. Inevitably, after a silent pause while she took bearings within, there was a gasp.

"Oh, Mr. Orum!" she cried, backing away from me. "What terrible deed have you done now? What is a lady to think? What is it that you carry around, what bloody remnant, in that sack?" She raised her voice: "Is it a murdered bairn?" Miss Speirs has a great taste for Tragical Enactments, and now she displayed all her fine skills in that art. Within moments, a crowd had gathered, wishing

---

51. It is clear that Mr. Orum's depravity affected his sense of honour, his duty to his wife, his responsibility to his children. What manner of man is it that looks, breathless, heart pounding, with Lust in his Loins, at another woman, when once he has married?

to see for themselves what horror I had concealed in the sack. There was nothing I could do but put my head down and – once more – run full tilt down the close, wondering as I fled, what manner of man I was.

———•———

Later that evening, after supper, I ventured once more to the mansion of Mr. Alexander Blair; this time, I took the sack with the Elephant's Brain contained within; for I had conceived a stratagem which would at once rid me of the Brain and at the same time release me from a perilous position in regard to my patron. Mr. Blair was at home, albeit indisposed, and, although he did not welcome my arrival on his door-step, neither did he turn me away. In the privacy of his bedroom, I put my proposition to him – the Brain, in exchange for the Foot. He was not at first kindly disposed to the trade, arguing that the Foot was far bigger, and therefore more consequential, than the Brain. But I counter-posed that it was not Quantity which should be considered here, but Quality: for, were we to remove an Elephant's foot, or a man's foot, then the Elephant or the man could still function well enough; but if we were to remove the Brain from either creature, then there would be no cure.

"Aye, well," mused Mr. Blair, pondering this universal truth, and adjusting his wig. "I am inclined to believe you, for I have seen such things in my time."[52]

---

52. With all respect to Mr. Blair, once Provost of Dundee, we do not believe that this is a 'universal truth'. We are acquainted with a keeper of chickens who has conducted convincing experiments on the negligible effects of the loss of a brain.

In short, Mr. Blair summoned his servant and we ex´changed the items, and Mr. Blair made haste to send me back out into the warm evening; he clutching the Brain wrapped in a cloth like some gigantic clootie´dumpling; myself with the heavy basket and the Foot contained safely therein. It stank. Even though my nose had now spent three days immersed in the meat and fluids of an Elephant, in one of the hottest weeks of Spring that Dundee had seen in this new century, I recognized that the left fore´foot of the Elephant reeked of corruption and of every malodorous gutter that had ever been neglected in the whole of Dundee. I know not what Mr. Blair had done with the item in the past two days, but he had cer´tainly not thought to keep it in a cool and dark place.

Barely had I entered my stair, than my neighbours opened their doors. To a man and a woman, they re´coiled at the stench. They discouraged me sternly from ascending any further; I retreated rapidly down the stair, followed closely by assorted lumps of wood, stones, and scraps of vegetable.

It was some time before I found a safe haven: I struck another deal with Mr. Campbell, that he would keep it safe for me in exchange for other items. But as I sit here now, in the silence of the night, I cannot rid my nostrils, or my hands, or clothes, of that over´powering odour of the grave: it is as if the foot were beside me. My children whimper in their sleep, Mrs. Orum will not have me in her bed, my mother stares out into the darkness with a look of profound disgust – but says nothing. My mind has taken to paths of its own. The Last Elephant stands in the corner, nodding contentedly.

4 MAY 1706.

On this Saturday, the fourth of May, seven nights having passed since the lamented *Florentia* fell upon the
road from Broughty Ferry, the day was again hot and the
River Tay, where it could be glimpsed between the reek
of the lums, sparkled under a blue heaven and the dark
shore of Fife.

At the very start of this day, Dr. Blair announced that
he had sent word to my brother Hendrie to come and
assist in the day's labour, which was likely to be hard.
Accordingly, after Hendrie's arrival, he and I and the
coarse servant Mr. Menteith, all straining hard, assisted
a carter in hauling a dyer's vessel from the cloth-works;
when Dr. Blair feels the need to boil up the bones of dead
beasts and the occasional innocent child, then he will use
a cauldron he keeps for that very purpose in his yard;
but for an Elephant something far more commodious is
required.

We built a huge fire-place in the yard, and started a fire
of rational size; Mr. Menteith rolled back his sleeves to
apply the bellows; it was Hendrie's task to fill the vat with
water from the pump; to which he applied himself with
great and visible enthusiasm. While we waited, it was the
heavy responsibility of Dr. Blair to examine the fruits of
my labours so far that week; making notes here on the
papers, or minor adjustments there, to what purpose I
could not tell, for my eye is sharp and my hand is steady:
what I observe, I draw, and there is nothing lost between
Nature and Depiction. But I am hardened to Dr. Blair's
habitual interference, and so ignored him: I know that

when I – and no one else – come to engrave the drawings
on to copper, I will distinguish between my own hand and
his hand, and engrave accordingly.

Late in the morning, the water finally came to the
boil, and we spent many hours thereafter as follows: at
the surgeon's command, I would feed the cauldron with
limbs and cuts of the Elephant; Hendrie would keep the
fire blazing and add more water; Mr. Menteith would stir
it all about and strain out the bones that were detached
by the action of the boiling water. Dr. Blair was a man
of great energy, hastening here and there, leaning on his
stick; he had abandoned his wig and coat, he moved about
in his shirt, his stringy hair blowing loose in the breeze; he
labelled the bones as they emerged steaming, measured
the amounts of oil which rose to the surface, issued orders
to his assistants; but found time to pat his young son on
the head when the latter made an appearance in the yard.
The whole scene was distasteful to me.

I was interrupted by a shout of warning from Menteith,
who saw that, as I thought pleasant thoughts of Miss
Samuella Speirs and Mrs. Hellen Orum to while away
the tedious hours, I was handing meaty bones to Hendrie,
and dropping firewood into the boiling water. I was so
tired, that I could scarce understand what Menteith was
telling me. I roused myself with the greatest of difficulty,
and paid attention to the matter of the day. Without
number were the pieces of meat we fed in; and without
number were the bones which were hauled out, excar-
nated, and ready for classification, categorisation and
philosophication. In went a head, without its brain, as
we know; and shortly afterwards, out came a skull, shreds
of boiled meat peeling from its several bones. The stench

was such that Dr. Blair's many neighbours, accustomed although they were to his peculiar ways, leaned upon the wall of the yard and remonstrated in low voices. None wished to anger the surgeon, for fear that he might not come to them in time of need, that they be left to die because they once complained of the smell from his ever-active cauldron. Philosophy has taken a firm grip around the throat of Dundee.

With the last rays of the sun casting low upon the Tay, we pulled out the final – that is to say, third – foot, with its bones dangling like those of an abandoned thief upon an old gibbet, strung together by rags likely to fall apart at the least puff of wind. Dr. Blair rubbed his hands in triumph. "Now," said he, "all I need do now is leave the Good Lord to shine His sun upon these bones during my day of rest, and I shall re-commence business on Monday." With that, he left us to clear away the boiled and useless meat, and to damp down the fire; we had instructions to carry the rich Elephant broth to a distant part of the harbour, and feed the fishes and pollute the seas therewith.

Hendrie, as is his way, was tired from the day's unaccustomed labour, and decided that we need not go so far; so he began to tip the greasy hot contents of the cauldron into the gutters of Scott's Close, the lane which runs outside the house. This last act raised a great noise in the district, for the broth was indeed sickly sweet and powerful. We barely escaped without a beating.

Abandoning my brother in the middle of this neighbourly dispute, I made best haste homewards, without stopping to visit any bakers or butchers or similar interested parties, my nostrils filled beyond redemption with the thick smoke and thicker brew. While my family sat in the far corner, handkerchiefs pressed to their dear little noses, I wrote in my Journal. Tonight, however, I will sleep. I will sleep.[53]

---

53. Let him sleep. The man has confessed himself to be on the verge of madness, brought on by lack of sleep, by innate depravity, no doubt also by falling into debt. We shall very shortly see how weak was his character, without the benefits of a Sound *Education*, the Backbone of *Religion* and the Guiding Light of *Thrift*.

5 MAY 1706.

As the surgeon had predicted, the sun today shone once more upon Dundee, the eighth day in succession. On a breeze from Scott's Close came the stench of the souring, hot broth of the previous evening, now bubbling like the Pox or Plague in the heat of the day. Such weather has never before been seen in our town. The sun shone doubtless upon Dr. Blair's yard, where the several hundred bones had been laid out neatly to dry. But my business on this Sabbath Day was not with Dr. Blair and his osteological numbers, but rather with my family. Taking advantage of the occasion and the weather, my wife and my children departed to take spiritual sustenance from Mr. Robertson, and I was left with my mother. I seized the opportunity to wash my head and hands in a tub of hot water, and scrape the Elephant from under my fingernails.

As we sat together, mother and son in comfortable silence, the Last Elephant stood in the corner and counted her own bones. She called them out; my mother nodded with great liveliness at each one; I noted them down as follows:

"My Head divided into those of the

    Upper Jaw, *viz.*

Calvaria, or upper and back part	1
Frons, or upper and fore part	1
Two *Maxillary* Bones	2
Two Bones of the Palate	2
Two *Zygomatic* Bones	2
Two *Styloid* Processes	2
Two Tusks	2
Four Grinders	4
Lower Jaw	1
Four Grinders	4
	21

My Trunk composed of the

    Spine consisting of the *Vertebrae* of the

Neck	7
Back	19
Loyns	3
Os Sacrum	5
Tail	29
Ribs, 19 Pairs	38
Sternum	4
	105

My Fore Extremities

Scapula	2
Humerus	2
Cubitus and *Radius*	4
Carpus, Six on each Foot	12
Metacarpus	12
Toes	24
Ossa Sesamoidea	24
	80

My Hind Extremities

    Ossa Innominata, *viz.*

Ilion and *Pubis*	2
Femur, or Thigh Bone	2
Tibia and *Fibula*, or Leg and Spit Bone	4
Patella, or Knee Pan	2
Tarsus	12
Metatarsus	12
Toes	20
	54 "

In total then, counted Philosophically: two-hundred-and-sixty bones.[54]

In the afternoon, young Agnes kindly offered to stay with her grand-mother and her brothers; while Mrs. Hellen Orum and I took a stroll down to the harbour, for to see the ships tied up. We had done this many times and more, and these precious few minutes of peace were normally an efficacious antidote to the troubles of the week. On this occasion, unfortunately, we were disturbed to find my brother and his friend Watty engaged in the sale of 'Elephant Meat'; this being the Sabbath, he did so with great circumspection. Anyone not familiar with Hendrie's ways would think that he and Watty were simply seated upon a barrel, taking the air. Such strips of meat as he had on sale were concealed within the bar-rel; he must have rescued them from Dr. Blair's yard; or maybe from the gutters of Scott's Close – I dared not ask. On seeing us approach, he had the decency to look embar-rassed, but to whisper to me with enthusiasm that the Heart was already sold twice over; after we had left him, he continued to offer his wares to an assembly of eager, but nervous, customers. We hastened away and came home by a different road.

After such a day, a man might expect to sleep soundly.

---

54. This, we find, is a most extraordinary Dream or Vision afforded to Mr. Orum. It is clear that he has lost his Mind. But what is less clear is how he came, from the depths of his delusions, to reproduce exactly and faultlessly, the very *Table of Bones* which Dr. Blair, four years later, printed on the 91st page of his Essay? If there be no Devilry here, then we must suppose Piracy. So much for Philosophical Arithmetic.

It is not to be: I sit here, under a moon which is the only light that I can afford.[55] I sit in my chair. The Last Elephant asks after Mr. Santos and Giovanni, and seems regretful that they have left for the warm countries. My smallest child wakes at the sound of our voices and calls my name. I whisper that all is well. All is not well; but I feel sleep coming upon me at last.

---

55. Ah – the Moon! Might its presence not offer us some explanation of Mr. Orum's delusions?

6 MAY 1706.

I slept for the rest of the night, and awoke this morning
to a cold haar that had crept off the Tay; it is my opinion
that the streaming cold air is far healthier for the people
of Dundee than the strong sun that stood in the sky in
the past week – the heat and unmoving air of summer is a
breeding pond for pestilence and disease, cooking up the
plague from Elephant broth – while the cold haar keeps
the humours in healthy balance. Many things I have chosen not to learn from Dr. Blair, but he and I were in complete agreement on this matter; as was Mr. Robertson the
preacher, for different reasons entirely. I made my way to
the surgeon's house, where he awaited my arrival with
some eagerness.

"Today," he said, "I will anatomize the Head."

I inclined my own head, an action which the surgeon
took for acquiescence, sought out my pen and paper, and
began to record the structure of the Elephant's Head.
One by one, the relevant pieces of bone were retrieved
from the drying pile in the yard, and, under Dr. Blair's
jealous eye, were examined, labelled, and represented on
paper. At last, after so many days of bestial toil, I was able
to exercise my art without significant interruption. Dr.
Blair had a great interest in the formation of the head – as
did I; for it must be said that the most prominent features
were attached to the head. Were man or woman to be furnished with such a long nose and such enormous teeth as
the Elephant, then the beast itself would be no great thing
to admire. Fortunately, I would argue, the trunk and the

tusks are in no way common in appearance among my fellow-men; at least, not in Dundee.

Since I have not travelled, I cannot tell what may be fashionable in England.

We began with the main part of the skull, which measured some three feet in diameter, and which had two eminences at either side of the front. Mr. Menteith stood back and voiced the coarse opinion that the two eminences reminded him of "Miss Gloag's **** – but nae sae big!"[56] I castigated him roundly, but he found support in his vulgar outburst from Dr. Blair, who laughed heartily and pointed out that "no less an authority on the Elephant than Mr. Ray has not unfitly compared them to a man's buttocks".[57] I know not who this Mr. Ray is, or was; but my judgement of him is poor, if his comparisons are so coarse; but never so coarse as Mr. Menteith's. When all mirth had died down, we returned to the more sober and responsible task of study.

We proceeded from these two eminences to a thorough examination and delineation of the various other holes and protuberances in that massive skull – the holes for

---

56. Neither Mr. Menteith – whose crude insult upon a part of a lady's anatomy must not go unremarked – nor Orum, who would have been better not remarking upon it, emerge from this small incident with any credit. Nor is it unambiguous which part of Miss Gloag's person is in question: we can only make a conjecture from a distant memory.

57. For his earthy humour, Dr. Blair must not be condemned. A man of great learning must be permitted to amuse as well as educate.

the eyes, for the root of the trunk, and for the tusks.[58] Dr.
Blair, as we studied the tusks, told us that the Elephant of
Dr. Moulins had had larger tusks than our specimen; but
our surgeon was not able to conclude whether this was a
result of the former being male and the latter female; or
the former being older, and the latter younger; or indeed,
of the tusks being broken, as appeared to be the case.
And, it seems, a German philosopher named Tentzelius[59]

58. We note that, in Dr. Blair's Essay of one hundred pages, no
fewer than six-and-twenty pages are devoted entirely to the Head
– the main part of the skull, the upper and lower jaw-bones, the
upper and lower teeth, the tusks, the sinus-holes, the internal parts
of the ear, the mechanism of the throat, the interior of the skull,
and so forth. The head of the Elephant is, we would argue, its most
momentous part. We will give you only some hint of the detail to
which our *fellow Dundonian* carried his investigation by quoting
the following short passage from his lengthy description of the
Jaw-bones:

"As the lower part of the Jaw in its Progress forward runs
obliquely downward, so its upper part of the Root of the Teeth runs
streight forward, or rather inclines a little upward so that whereas
'tis on 6½ Inches from above to below at the joining of the Teeth,
now 'tis 7½ Inches streight downward […] Now we consider the
inner part of the Place where we left it, and find it still more plain;
where measuring from below the foresaid joining of the two Teeth
streight forward, 'tis 4 Inches on each side, till both meet in a
Semicircle about 3 Inches Diameter at the lower part, and somewhat
nearer at the Root of the Teeth. After it has run 2 Inches upward, it
runs streight forward with a convex Surface 4 Inches thick; thence it
ascends 4 Inches more to the Root of the Teeth."

With his facility of words, Dr. Blair once more brings the
Elephant to life!

59. Dr. Blair advises us that Dr. Moulins and Dr. Tentzelius were

has alleged that the tusks on some Elephants were said to be up to eight feet long, and weigh one hundred pounds, or even twice as much, that from such tusks were made door-posts. In a flight of my imagination, I wondered whether the Princes of India might perhaps build great palaces from the skulls and tusks of dead Elephants. I made the mistake of expressing this thought aloud – if I have a weakness in company, it is to say things that need not be said; Dr. Blair made no reply, but expressed his own opinion that perhaps the Lords of Scotland, when they had sold the nation into bondage, might make palaces of the buttocks of the men they had sold.[60] The mirth of Mr. Menteith was uncontrolled at this startling image. There are two kinds of men in the world: those who find everything – good or evil, comic or tragic – a subject for mirth; and those who do not.[61]

In all of this long day, I was pleased that my employer did not call upon me to do any more than exercise my natural talents, and so I was at liberty to make exact drawings of every aspect of the skull.[62] It was with an uncommon

---

the fore-most Authorities on the matters Elephantine; of course, our *Dundonian Hippocrates* now towers over these two by far.

60. We are much amused by this thought; clearly, Dr. Blair was in good humour this day!

61. We should not wonder at Orum's penny-market Philosophy: he is not a man of any wisdom or morality. Mr. Orum, there are two kinds of men in this world: those who sleep well; and those who do not.

62. It is with a heavy heart, and only from a *Christian* Duty, that we will acknowledge that Mr. Orum's engravings were later incorporated into Dr. Blair's Essay. Our apothecary-surgeon,

sentiment of satisfaction, therefore, that I packed away my instruments at the end of that day, and made my way back to my home, stopping, on the road, to refresh the memories of several trades-men of my recent favours to them. I found that Mr. Dalrymple, the merchant of vegetables, was open to trade with me on being offered a small piece of tongue; in similar manner, and with a similar item, did I trade for cheese with Mr. Montgomery, the dairy-man. The shop of Mr. Sutherland, however, was once more closed at an early hour – a strange action indeed for a man interested in the sale of candles.

However, I preferred not to engage in idle speculation about his lack of interest in trade; and hurried on, bearing potatoes, cheese and a small morsel of fish for my family.

Before I reached the safety of my home, I noticed that something was amiss on the streets of Dundee. There was an illness abroad. Men and women were lying on the ground, eyes staring wildly, from the depths of the closes there were shouts of insane laughter and dangerous reels were performed in and out of house-entrances. From the windows of tenements came showers of fleas, straw and feathers, as women pulled apart bedding and hurled it

---

however, has this to say about them:

"Tho' the draughts of the Engraver be course, yet I have endeavoured what in me lay to have the Figures true and well-proportion'd";

and further, that:

"the Copper Plates, which at my own Charges I have caused to be engraven here, I acknowledge might have been done finer in London."

So much for our master-engraver!

to the breeze. In the gutter, filthy with ordure, a respect-able clerk wrestled like a lion with a broad woman of low repute, the pair of them utterly naked and silent. I beheld old Mr. Douglas, from a cough barely able to continue his trade as coffin-maker, circling energetically on one foot, while he whistled powerfully to the seagulls above. I met Mrs. Speirs, who greeted me with an embrace and a kiss full upon my lips, causing me to drop my potatoes, before she burst into tears and sat down suddenly upon the ground, lamenting that her bonny lad had left her, no more a maiden. A cart, laden with and pushed by weav-ers, having no horse in attendance, hurtled down the lane, while those aboard shouted "o'er the hill, o'er the sea!", until finally cart, passengers and three accompanying dogs careered into the wall of the kirkyard and flew in among the grave-stones, screaming with laughter.

It was as if Dundee had in a day become a Bedlam. And then I met my brother Hendrie, hiding in the shad-ows with a broad grin upon his face. "Aye-aye, Gibby," said he in a satisfied tone, "yon Elephant-meat has a fair kick, eh?" I hurried home, found my family unaffected, and locked my door. As I write, there is still an air of fes-tivity in the streets outside: the night is filled with the laughter, sobs and screams of dissipation.[63]

---

63. Accepting our responsibility as Editor with the utmost gravity, we have investigated Orum's strange tale, and we can confirm that no document, letter or report bears witness to such an episode in the history of the sober citizens of Dundee. So much for Bedlam.

8 MAY 1706.

Yesterday, the seventh day of May, Dr. Blair drove us to philosophize the Legs of the Elephant. Under the surgeon's superintendence, we re-assembled the pile of bones that made up the foot; and measured each; and noted down all of our measurements. We found and fitted the Humerus and the Cubitus and the Radius. We studied and measured the Carpus. Then we moved in upon the External Bone of the first Rank, the second Bone of the first Rank, the third Bone of the first Rank; having exhausted those items, we passed to the first Bone of the second Rank, the second Bone of the second Rank, and the third Bone of the second Rank. Next, and with a pause only for a rapid dinner, we came to the first, second, third, fourth, fifth, and – without any great surprise – sixth bones of the Metacarpus.

My feelings during this entire procedure were ones of distaste. Dr. Blair presumed, having dismembered the Elephant, to set it to rights again, without any respect at all for the beast which, only ten days earlier, had paced with its huge feet the same Earth as ourselves. Dr. Blair urged me to work faster; my hand ached with my drawing; I said so with some heat; I said also that the beast deserved some care and respect, now that it had died. His only response was to turn to his slave Menteith, and, in a cold manner, state that he had re-named the third Bone of the second Rank: "hereinafter, Mr. Menteith, it shall be called the *Ossiculum Orumiculum Inutilum*." Having little Latin, I could only guess at the meaning of this jibe; Mr. Menteith pretended to understand fully. I found tears in

my eyes, but continued my careful work: I have determined that my engravings of this poor Elephant will far
out-live any notes made by Dr. Blair.[64]

As the day drew to a close, Dr. Blair philosophized the
Toes of the Elephant. When we had exhausted the front
legs and front foot, he turned to look at the pile of bones,
now greatly diminished, and then stretched in a satisfied
manner. "The hind quarters," he announced, "may wait
until the morrow. How would that be, Miss Gloag?"

The cook had much to say on the matter, her humour
not greatly lightened by the events of the day, nor by her
unexpected failure to acquire more candles from Mr.
Sutherland's shop, which, it seemed, remained closed.
Miss Gloag expressed herself in the following terms:
"Yon is a dowf ******* and a ***** ****, and I dinna
care who kens it, Dr. Blair."

Dr. Blair sent us all home. I packed up my instruments
of trade, and left them in a press in the kitchen, along with
all the drawings and his note-books; for they would all be
required on the following day. And then I went out into a
cold, dull afternoon.

As I passed the door of Mr. Sutherland's shop, I hesitated. I pondered whether I might, in inadvertent manner, have been the cause of some fatal accident behind
that closed door. I looked up and down the close, then
chapped loudly upon the wood. There was some kind of
noise within, but no answering voice. I chapped again,

---

64. A false hope, we suppose. Dr. Blair's conclusive Study of an
Elephant was printed by the Royal Society in 1710, to great acclaim.
Orum's engravings are preserved for posterity only because of the
fame of Dr. Blair.

louder, calling out Mr. Sutherland's name. I believe it might have been the sound of my voice that roused the chandler; for there was a clatter, as of stools falling over, a grunt, then a rush of foot-steps; the door was thrown open. Mr. Sutherland stood there, unshaven, hair wild, coat unbuttoned; he was flushed around the throat and blood-shot in the eye; his hands shook.

"Mr. Orum," said he, in a hoarse voice. "Is it yerself, then?"

"Indeed," I affirmed. "I was concerned for your good health –"

He interrupted me. "Dinna concern yerself wi' that!" he exclaimed. "Dae ye have anything for me – ye ken, anything at all for me, in the way of ..." He did not finish his sentence in words, merely with some crazed nods and winks. By which I understood that he might refer to some *Partes Generationi Inservientes*, such as I had provided before. I told him that I had no more just now.

"But ye'll remember me if ye get more, eh, Mr. Orum?" he demanded eagerly, seizing me by the collar, and pouring his foul breath upon me. In order to effect an escape, I assured him that he would be given first choice of anything in that line, prised myself from his grip, and hastened down the close; content, at least, to know that the man was not yet dead. As I left, he thrust into my arms some good-sized candles, such as might light up a kirk; he expected, no doubt, some compensating return.

The vennels and closes of Dundee resounded yet to the unaccustomed sounds of frantic and unbridled delight, laughter yet followed fast upon shrieks of horror, men, both young and old, still strutted in the streets, their eyes burning with visions, their mouths full of tongues. The

respectable wives of merchants were to be found stagger-
ing as if intoxicated, in gangs of four and five, threatening
passing strangers with embrace, intimacy or a cut throat.
Hendrie, it would seem, had been at his trade again. Mr.
James Robertson was abroad, patrolling his parish with
more than common enthusiasm, a smile – such as we have
not seen in twenty years – upon his lips: he raised his hat
as I passed, observing that the Lord was surely speak-
ing to each and every man and woman of Dundee. "Mr.
Orum," said he, "we have been in Egyptian captivity ere
now; now we are set free!" With that, he walked swiftly
forwards.

My wife was greatly pleased with the new candles, and
we lit them as soon as darkness fell upon Dundee; then
my daughter sang a number of Psalms in a reedy voice. I
wrote what little needed to be written in my journal, then
gained my bed.

In the middle of the night, I was brought slowly awake
by the realisation that the Last Elephant was talking to
me in a low voice, a rumble only. The Elephant said that
she was burning. I sat up and saw, to my horror, that one
of Sutherland's candles, which I thought to have snuffed
properly, had smouldered on past midnight; and had now,
unattended, set light to the Elephant. The blazing beast
paced in agitation around the room, dropping as she did
so small fires on everything she passed; the wood of the
rafters was beginning to smoke and burn. I leaped from
my bed and attacked the fires with the contents of the
bed-pan; but to no avail; for, just as I threw the few drops,
so the roof caught light and began to blaze.

The house was now on fire. My children awoke and
screamed. My wife hid under the blanket. My mother

asked me whether "the English have come with torches to smoke us out, Gibby?"; and then she shrieked with delight.

There was no time to be lost. I seized my children and ran with them to the top of the stair. There I shouted to warn all my neighbours that the house was afire, and that all should now flee. This advice was swiftly acted upon and we reached the confines of the close outside in the company of some hundred of our neighbours, themselves screaming, laughing and cursing. Some, certainly, considered the fire to be just another delusion of their fevered minds, another entertainment for their lost souls; others were less sure. Far above us, we could see the flames bursting through the roof; the sound of crackling soon overwhelmed our voices, and showers of falling sparks poured upon our heads. My wife had made her own way down; and I returned for my mother. She sat in her bed, her eyes alive and flickering with the reflected flames, trapped in fascination; I seized her and, ignoring her scolding, brought her to safety. The Elephant followed. Some women from the stair had by then had the good sense to arrange for buckets of water to be fetched, and soon a line of men was rushing up the steps to pour water upon the flames. For my part, I could do nothing, so tightly did my wife and children have me in their grip; and so we stood and watched as the fire was fought.

At last, as the dawn approached, some order was restored. The efforts of my neighbours – and of their neighbours, justifiably concerned that the burning of one building would lead, as it frequently does, to the burning of their own building – had not been in vain; and although the tenement was drier than it commonly was at that time of year, only the top two floors had been burned out. Unfortunately, this meant that my family no longer had a home. We had escaped with our lives, our blankets, and not much else besides.[65]

———•———

As dawn broke, the noise of the fire and of its spectating attendants had reached my brother's ears, and he came looking for excitement; he was much sobered to find that my family was in such a state; and immediately proposed that we come and stay with him. "Aye, come on: there's plenty of room, ye ken," said he, without any regard for the truth. My wife and children looked at me in terror, for they knew what awaited them there – a dark clarty room, occupied by a dozen wild children, ruled over a bitter and heavy-handed woman. But there was nothing else we could do. There was little hope in asking my neighbours for refuge. Most of them had no room for their own families.

"The bairns will be glad of the company," added Hendrie, threateningly.

My mother refused this invitation absolutely. "I will not," said she in a loud voice, "I will not go with that man. He is a fool. He is a rascal. And his family are the Spawn of the Devil." I noticed that several neighbours nodded in agreement at this judgement. With a heavy heart, I sent off my wife and my poor children to the care of Hendrie and his family. All cried bitter tears, as if taking ship to America or Darien, never to return.

---

65. Such, we are obliged to remark, Gentlemen, are the *Wages of Sin.*

I was abandoned in the close with my mother; who glared at me in expectation. In my desperation, I considered that the Reverend Robertson, who had a great admiration for my mother, and who tolerated her many weaknesses, might be persuaded to find shelter for us; and so I made my way to the manse. The house-keeper was not willing to let us in; but Mr. Robertson came to see what was the disturbance, and was very kind to us. He was greatly sympathetic when he heard of our troubles; and found a straight-backed chair in which my mother might rest; the house-keeper was reminded of her Christian duty; and was imposed upon to provide my mother with a strong draught; my mother stared at the house-keeper stony-eyed, and refused to have anything to do with her or to drink the restorative; the house-keeper was affronted; I was ashamed.

Mr. Robertson and I discussed my position.

"Alas," he said, "your mother cannot stay here long, for some men of strong faith are expected in Dundee imminently, to witness these great marvels; I shall need all the beds in the house."[66]

I nodded, waiting for some spark of hope to light up the sable darkness of the day. Mr. Robertson pondered,

---

66. Despite the rumours that associated him with the *Radicals* of Dundee, the Reverend Robertson was noted by all who knew him as a man of *Sound Sense* and *Christian Goodness*. Assuredly, had an assembly of fellow-ministers not been expected, he would have accommodated all of Mr. Orum's family, despite the engraver's notoriety. We have, we expect, all been in a similar position, when our profound wish to act as a Good Samaritan is frustrated by some other obligation. In this way do we temper our *Moral* and our *Social* duties.

gazing out of his window upon his small orchard of ap-
ple-trees, which were then in blossom. Mingled with the
white blossom which had fallen to the ground was the fine
ash from a fire nearby.

"The Lord would say," he said at last, "that Dr. Blair
should be reminded of his Christian Duty. He has a large
house, has he not? His soul will greatly profit from having
a man of your godliness at his side. Aye," he said, cutting
short my protests, "aye, in God's truth, that would be
best. Let us go down to that godless man this very instant,
and set now his feet upon the path of Righteousness."

With great enthusiasm, which it would be uncharitable to view as revenge, the minister took me off to
Crichton-street.

The Blair family were at breakfast, much startled to
see me arrive so early, even more so to find Mr. Robertson
upon the threshold.

"Ah!" said Dr. Blair, before he had had the time to
establish the facts, "I dare say you are eager for Philosophy
this morning, Mr. Orum?"

Mr. Robertson soon acquainted him with the facts,
and while the pair of them fell into useless argument,
Mrs. Blair arranged that my mother and I should occupy
a spare room in the attic, which had once been used for a
servant, but was no longer required. Mrs. Blair would tend
to my mother's immediate needs, and the pair of us could
be fed at the family table, until such time as new lodgings
could be found for the whole family. The surgeon, seeing
that the matter was settled, said nothing about rent; but
I saw all the profits from this engagement slipping away,
like the purse from the hand of a dying man.

Such, I heard the voice of my conscience whisper to me, are the Wages of Sin.

———•———

I should, I suppose, have experienced a stronger sensa' tion of gratitude; indeed, for several minutes after Mr. Robertson's triumphant departure, I was seized with an over'powering desire to confess to Dr. Blair the secret of the missing Metacarpus and Carpus and to make a full confession, to unburden myself of all that drove me. However, having been dispatched back to our home to see if any possessions could be salvaged, I soon realized that I could do no such thing. Far better, I thought, to stumble upon the missing item as if by a great cast of fate, and gain the gratitude of the surgeon by this one piece of unlooked'for good fortune.

At our tenement, I managed with terror to gain entry to our room. The scene was one of utter devastation. All that could burn, had burned; all that could tumble from a height and be smashed, had duly done so. Only by the greatest chance had a number of items of dress been pre' served from the fire; I bundled these up and took them to my family in Hendrie's room. It was as if I had brought shrouds as gifts for condemned prisoners: my children burst into tears, and my wife sat hopelessly in a corner; while Margaret, Hendrie's wife, regarded us all with the narrowed eyes of disapproval. On her fire, a pot bubbled: the smell was of Elephant meat – I feared for the well' being of my family.[67]

---

67. We have every sympathy for Mrs. Orum and her children, but none for the man.

Once outside in the air, I went to retrieve the fore-foot from Mr. Campbell, with whom I had left it just a few nights before.

To my horror, the fish-monger denied that I ever gave it to him, that he ever had it, that he knew where it was. He threatened to expose me, should I pursue the matter. The man is a scoundrel. He chased me from his shop.

I sit here in Dr. Blair's house, writing in my journal, and await the final crushing blow of fate, for surely I am undone.[68]

---

68. At last – Mr. Orum's conscience stirs! The delinquent must suffer as he sees his crimes unravel, as he sees the inexorable *Juggernaut* of Justice bearing down upon him! How many men have felt as Orum does, as they step to the scaffold?

9 MAY 1706.

After that terrible fire, and the destruction of all our possessions, Dr. Blair was considerate enough, I suppose,
to allow that I should not have to work on the Elephant
today. As it happens, the surgeon's enthusiasm for his
philosophical investigation had kept him from his usual
patients and cares; and he himself made shift to set off
on such surgical business as awaited in him in the town
of Dundee on the Tay. His daily business is the sewing-
up of heads, the sawing-off of legs, the administration
of vegetable purgatives, all manner of necessary evils;
which does not prevent Dr. Blair, upon his return from
such adventures, from enlightening his family, guests and
attendants on the transactions of the day, with particular
attention to sanguineous details. At times, he will have
with him an apprentice, Mr. John Butler, who seems to
have little mind of his own, but a great thirst for the words
of his teacher.[69] Mr. John Butler, it need not be said, did

---

69. Our tireless investigations, to which we have alluded before,
have revealed that this same Mr. Butler, himself by that time a
surgeon, died tragically in Arbroath in 1709. It was a curious
incident: Mr. Butler had been instrumental in establishing a 'Grand
Natural History Philosophy Club' in that town. One windy day,
he walked beside the sea with a fellow of the Club, discussing the
natural history of 'smokies'. As they reached the summit of a sand-
dune, an Oyster-Catcher, borne swiftly by the gale off the sea, of
a sudden flew up and collided with Mr. Butler. The bird's orange
bill penetrated Mr. Butler's right ear. Both man and bird died
instantaneously. The Oyster-Catcher was stuffed and mounted and
now sits in pride of place within the rooms of the 'Grand Natural

not concern himself once with the investigation of the Elephant, his spirit, perhaps, inhabited and moved by far more elevated thoughts.

Today I was entirely occupied with two oppressive problems: firstly, trying to find a new home for my family; and secondly, trying to find the missing extremity of the Elephant. In the former endeavour, I had no worries for my mother, who made herself as comfortable in Dr. Blair's house as anyone could have wished. Some distraction for her was provided by young Master John Blair, the unfortunate son of the surgeon, who developed an immediate fascination with my mother's presence in the narrow attic-room which had been allocated to us; despite his mother's prayers and scoldings, he insisted on climbing to the threshold of the room, pushing the door slightly ajar and gazing with wide eyes upon the figure of my mother as she lay upon the bed muttering, or as she paced the floor in her night-shirt, her greasy hair tangled like that of a witch, watching, from the tiny window, the roof-tops of Dundee for any sign of fire. Noticing the presence of the young lad, she soon enticed him into her world, where dreams and nightmares and the fantastical spilled their hot breath upon the cold dull stones of the house. Young John was easily excited; and my mother and he spend hours together in wanton amusement.

I fear these few hours of consorting with my mother may have done the boy untold harm; I know that my years with her have ruined my own life. Young John's mother has many cares at this time, and is unable to keep an eye

---

History Philosophy Club' of Arbroath; Mr. Butler does not. So much for Natural History.

on her son at every minute of the day; she tries to dissuade him from unwise conventions; but is not greatly assisted in this endeavour by her husband's undisciplined espousal of experimentation and discovery; and his consequent encouragement of his son in philosophical investigation of God's more enigmatical creations.

The matter was far less easy for my dear wife and children, whose presence I miss greatly. I paid them a visit three times today – but it was as if they had been locked away in the Tolbooth, for there seemed to be no hope of escape from the tireless disturbance and provocations of Hendrie's children, the oppressive glances of Margaret, nor the chafing good intentions of Hendrie himself. I visited morning, noon, and night; and on each occasion I saw my family wilt before me, as if they had been flowers plucked and left to perish upon a grave. I was unable to find a room in which we could live, at a rent which we might afford. And so tonight we sleep apart.

———◆———

And secondly, as I say, I must needs establish the present situation of the missing fore-foot. While I may not be so greatly moved by Dr. Blair's hospitality that I wish to retrieve and restore the missing item forthwith; I have at least the duty to establish what the perfidious Campbell has done with it; and to put myself once again in such a position that its convenient return will be at my command. An Elephant without one fore-foot is, we may be sure, an Elephant incomplete; and while it is not my business to ensure that Dr. Blair's proposed Osteology is complete in all particulars, I have my own good reason to ensure that every Last Elephantine part is recovered.

Nor am I like to forget that the foot is missing, for the surgeon refers to its absence at almost every opportunity. "The Elephant is," he declaimed this morning early, "in the position of the nation of Scotland: flayed, boiled, laid bare and – for all that – not even perfect in death. I must," he encouraged us all, "find that missing foot."

To which end, spies were sent out today into the streets of Dundee and the lanes of Broughty Ferry: Miss Gloag was encouraged to gossip – encouragement being scarcely necessary – with fellow-cooks and house-keepers in the shops and the fish-market; Mr. Menteith was sent out in disguise, to drink and make merry among the scum of the earth and the criminal classes – I am certain that he passed inspection without the slightest difficulty; I myself was engaged to listen out for any rumour which might lead to the discovery of the item. Dr. Blair suggested that my brother be recruited as well; but then he reminded himself of Hendrie's character; and decided against it. As for Mr. Butler, he was instructed to pay attention as he went around the sick and the extreme of Dundee, and to speak softly into the ears of the dying, to ask if any last confession might be forthcoming on the matter; Mr. Butler undertook this most willingly; but I wonder how it must have appeared to those unfortunate people who – about to draw their last breath in this disappointing world; and expectant of words of higher import to accompany them to Heaven or to Hell – found themselves drifting into oblivion with questions on the missing left fore-foot of an Elephant; perhaps they imagined that they had already passed the Portals of Death, and that the questions now whispered in their ear were the commencement of a thousand years of Damnation; or that they now stood at the Gates to Heaven, being quizzed in matters of religion; and now – too late – bitterly repented their lack of attention in the kirk.[70]

Neither Miss Gloag, nor Mr. Menteith, nor Mr. Butler met with any success, although they did, without doubt, amuse themselves greatly in the attempt. As for myself, I went about my researches with considerable preparation, fore-thought and circumspection. Mr. Campbell, on being challenged, led me behind his cloth curtain and demonstrated that the foot was not there: I must suppose that he had sold it to another. My suspicions were then directed at the other trades-men with whom I had so far made contracts on matters relating to the Elephant. Masking my intentions under the appearance of conducting daily business with them, I paid visits upon Mr. Dalrymple the vegetable-merchant, Mr. Seton the butcher and – with considerable trepidation – Mr. Sutherland the supplier of candles. Not one of them yielded any useful information. The eyes of Mr. Sutherland were furtive enough, but I gave that little thought, for he is a man whose eyes are never other than furtive – and it was clear from his demeanour that he had far more questions to ask of me than I had of him. For his part, Mr. Seton was anxious to know if I had access to the liver of the Elephant, since "I have an interested customer, Mr. Orum". In order not to

---

70. Mr. Orum's grasp of theological truths is lamentable. Only those of little education would mistake a question concerning an Elephant with the *Greater Questions* of Death and Eternal Life. We fully expect to be asked far more profound questions at that Everlasting Instant; and we have prepared ourselves accordingly with the answers.

lose his attention, for I should have further need of his
good humour, I prevaricated and suggested that "perhaps
something could be done, Mr. Seton". At these words,
the butcher rubbed his hands in happy anticipation, and
his son emulated him with uncanny precision; it was a
wonder to behold how many trades are handed down,
father to son, and with them, the manners and expres-
sions that enhance the trade. I am pleased to say that I
exhibit nothing of my father's behaviour, whatever my
mother might have to say on the subject. I wonder what
my own children will make of themselves.[71]

I called this afternoon upon another business acquaint-
ance of mine, Mr. Lockhart the blacksmith, who supplies
me with sheets of copper on which to etch my engravings.
Mr. Lockhart is a silent, dour man, native of Pickletillum
in Fife; who had made the voyage to Dundee to seek his
fortune in the year of 1689, imagining that the change of
the King might herald grand new times for the people
of Scotland. In this he was mistaken; nevertheless he
managed to pick up some trade in the flourishing town
to which he had been ferried. This was due in most part,
it has to be admitted, to his natural skills in shaping and
beating metal. Mr. Lockhart, aside from his daily trade

71. Not, we fear, very much: our Dunfermline correspondent, now
a frozen corpse in Canada, advised us that: the daughter Agnes went
off to Edinburgh to seek a fortune or a husband in the grand houses
there, and married a rat-catcher; young Hendrie found the trade
of weaving greatly to his taste and consequently died in poverty
in 1722; Thomas went off to fish, and was soon drowned; and the
youngest son, Robert, joined the Navy – it is a relief to find that at
least one scion of Orum did more than gripe and complain, and went
off to serve his Country. So much, however, for Children,

of horse-shoes, pans and pots, cauldrons and gates, was pleased to produce items of 'a more gentle sort', such as candle-sticks, decorated bed-warmers, or ornamented rain-spouts for kirk-roofs; this last item being in frequent demand, despite the strict avoidance of godlessness within the kirk, as Mr. John Knox had ordained, and which prohibition was eagerly pursued by many of the ministers of these parts; nevertheless, since a kirk-roof has to have some device to shed the rain which beats upon it, or else collapse under the weight of the down-pour, it may – according to some of the more Episcopalian persuasion – it may as well be a device that warns sinners of the creatures that would await them in the realm of eternal rain.

I approached Mr. Lockhart with the entirely convincing excuse that I would shortly require from him some sheets of good-quality copper, on to which I would transfer my drawings of the Elephant. Mr. Lockhart – doubtless like every man, woman and child in Dundee – had heard of the great work being undertaken at Dr. Blair's house; and was keen to learn more. More particularly, Mr. Lockhart was anxious to learn of the shapes and articulations of the various bones of the Elephant. It was soon clear that Mr. Lockhart had had a moment of inspiration, which was this: if he were to make some candle-sticks in shape and form alike to recognizable parts of the deceased Elephant of Dundee; then he would find a ready market among the richer people of the land, "perhaps even as far as Perth, would you say, Mr. Orum?" he asked me, "Would you say that they have heard of our Elephant there?" I assured him that such news travels wide and fast.

"So, Mr. Orum," asked Mr. Lockhart, seizing me by my sleeve, and drawing me closer to his beard than

I felt was appropriate, "do you think that you could, in exchange maybe for a slight lowering of my prices in the matter of the copper, get me some examples of these bones?"

From this request, it was evident that Mr. Lockhart was innocent of the theft of the foot.

These words were more than I had ever heard Mr. Lockhart speak at one time in the dozen years that I had known him; it was clear to me that he felt a passion about this enterprise of his; it was, it should be admitted, an enterprise of some promise. In every comfortable home, a merchant and his family could gather under the light of candles held aloft by the mighty *Scapula* of the Elephant; or a Minister and his flock might say the Lords' Prayer more devoutly than would normally be the case, if their kirk was lit by candles held in iron replicas of the *maxillary* bones of the Elephant; an ordinary man might even invest in a pair of decorative candle-snuffers shaped after the manner of the Tusks, and so ensure the safety of his home.

But – how am I to acquire bones for Mr. Lockhart? Already, Dr. Blair has instituted intensive searches for one missing fore-foot; he has his notes and my drawings of every part of the Elephant which we had so far studied; and he is a man who has intimate knowledge of the skeletons of every animal and child which has died within ten miles of Dundee – he would detect immediately the absence of just one small toe or rib. Mr. Lockhart is, however, a very strong man, as befits his profession; and not one whom a more philosophical artist can easily deny. With a small measure of deceit, therefore, I indicated to the black-smith that I would look out some suitable bone for him, citing the mighty *metasternal* bone, the *zygomatic tusk-bone* and the *os auditorius* as my preferred choices for his 'gentler' work. He seemed greatly satisfied with this; and assured me that he would have my plates of copper ready for me within the week. He clasped my hand in his, compressed every *metacarpus* that resides therein, and smote me between the *Scapulae* to seal the bargain.

I have no great idea how I am to deliver on my promises; but suppose that, since I have presently the freedom almost of Dr. Blair's house, it might be possible to uncover some forgotten skeleton somewhere; and relieve it of a bone or two of appropriate dimensions and weight. Surely there is a dead boar under the stairs, or a circus-bear in the out-houses? Perhaps, however, another stratagem would serve: Dr. Blair has the notes, but I have the drawings. Could I re-work one of my drawings, and remove a bone; or replace, in my drawing, an Elephant's bone with that of another animal? Dr. Blair would be none the wiser, Mr. Lockhart would have his bone.[72]

---

72. Are we to believe, then, that Dr. Blair would not notice such a blatant deception? We think not. Or are we to suppose that Mr. Orum's drawings, poor things that they are, contain the representations of an animal other than the *Dundee* Elephant? Is his so-called Last Elephant a *Chimera*, a mockery of God's natural creations?

10 MAY 1706.

I slept poorly in Dr. Blair's house. I crept downstairs at midnight to examine by candlelight some of my drawings, in search of one which could be re-worked in favour of Mr. Lockhart. But my ill-luck with candles continued when, engrossed in my studies, I failed to notice that my night-shirt had caught afire. With some difficulty, I cast it from me and stamped it out upon the tiles. The noise of my trouble attracted the attentions of Miss Gloag, who slept close by, and I was obliged to retreat, leaving her only the smell of smoke and a glimpse of a naked man fleeing the scene of his mis-fortune. This morning she remarked caustically upon this unusual circumstance to Dr. Blair; he raised an eye-brow, and ventured no opinion. Mr. Menteith hazarded a guess which came uncomfort-ably close to the truth, and added an amatory dimension to his story, which amused his master, but ill-pleased me. I have disposed of my night-shirt in the midden.

Dr. Blair began today to pine for his osteological work, and summoned me and Mr. Menteith to re-commence our study of the skeletal remains.

"I have progressed," he reminded us, "only so far as the front legs. Mr. Menteith, I think we should advance with some passion upon the hind-quarters."

Mr. Menteith snickered coarsely, as I knew he would, and as Dr. Blair expected. Miss Gloag was wise enough by now to be nowhere near at hand, else she would have had considerable fuel for her usual invective.

We fell almost immediately upon the *Pelvis*, which, being in circumference some four feet and six inches, is, in

Dr. Blair's estimation, 'of considerable bigness'. To this bone are attached all manner of other important parts.[73] From the *Pelvis* we passed down to the hind legs, where first we encountered the *Femur*, one of the largest bones, being three feet in length in our specimen. Mr. Lockhart, it is sure and certain, would give a King's Ransom for such a bone; and, were it mine to acquire it for him, I would gladly have done so; and gained a friend for life. From this higher bone in the leg, we came to the *Patella* or knee-bone: "a bone of very rugous surface," we were advised by our learned dissector, "considerably protuberant on the outside"; and thence to the *Tibia* and the *Fibula*, which form the lower part of the leg. All of which, according to Dr. Blair, was quite straight-forward; being in no way different in the Elephant than it is in many another creature of the land. I was not glad to hear this, for, when it was a matter of 'simple' construction of the osteology, then Dr. Blair would gallop through the study; and would demand that I hasten through my drawings thereof; without at the same time losing any of the required exactitude. Such speed led to considerable cramping in my right hand.

---

73. Indeed, Mr. Orum has observed – for once – correctly: Dr. Blair has this to say in his Essay:

"These Ossa Innominata are flat before, standing almost perpendicular with the two lower and utmost extremities of the Os Ilion bending forward, having the Os Pubis ascending obliquely, convex before, where join'd together, and concave behind. This ascent of the Os Pubis is a further Argument, that this is no Retrocoitent Animal."

We remain uncertain as to the proper names of the Ossa Innominata, and would encourage any surgical gentleman to contribute to our knowledge of these.

It was with considerable relief, then, that our efforts were interrupted by the arrival of Mr. George Yeaman.[74] He had come to collect the promised skin, which had, for the past two days, been lying stinking in a corner of the yard. Mr. Yeaman and Dr. Blair exchanged some guarded pleasantries; and then Mr. Yeaman expressed an interest to see what had become of the rest of 'his' Elephant; Dr. Blair was observed to raise his eye-brows at Mr. Yeaman's proprietorial tone; but made no direct remark on it, beyond some references of his own to the skin of the Elephant "now in your possession" and the bones "now in my possession".

After a few short minutes, it was evident that Mr. Yeaman had little interest in the philosophical dissection of the Elephant, but wished to sound out Dr. Blair on the matter of his – Mr. Yeaman's – chances in the election to Provost. "I have great hopes," he added, "that, on being elected the next Provost of Dundee, I will shortly there-after take up a seat in the new Parliament at Westminster in London."

"Indeed?" observed Dr. Blair coolly. "Is it not a little premature to be considering a seat in London before our patriotic Commissioners have even completed their de-bate? What if they decide that Scotland shall have no seats at all at Westminster?"

Mr. Yeaman laughed. "I suppose that we need have no fear that the Commissioners will act in the best interests

---

74. We have previously made observations on this Pillar of Society and *Hercules of Dundee*. Just this once, we are grateful to Mr. Orum for this unique vignette of a Truly Great Dundonian, here in his element.

of Scotland, Dr. Blair."

Dr. Blair nodded at length. "Certainly, Mr. Yeaman, certainly. There is no doubt in my mind that they will reach the conclusion for which they are paid."

In Dr. Blair's estimation, as I knew after several days in his close company, the Commissioners for the Treaty of Union were quite simply traitors who would sell out the interests of Scotland for promises of their own personal advantage. It was clear that Mr. Yeaman knew precisely what was meant by Dr. Blair's words; but, no doubt seeking a vote, he did not rise to the challenge.

"I would suggest," continued our visitor, "that the present state of Scotland is much the same as the present state of my Elephant there."

"In what way, I wonder?" asked Dr. Blair.

"In the following way: that Scotland, after the ill-advised adventure of the Scottish African Company to the land of Darien, is no longer capable of making her way in the world of trade. That what is best for the people of Scotland is to take the body apart and examine it closely to see how the death of our trade was arrived at; and then, with the help of our friends in London, to put together a new skeleton on which the meat of a flourishing oeconomy may hang. That our future, in short, Dr. Blair, lies in reaching a Treaty of Union with England."

Dr. Blair pondered these opinions for a few moments. "Mr. Yeaman," he replied at length, "I can only concur that the present state of Scotland is comparable to my poor Elephant; it has been ridden to death by those who had only their own interests at heart; and, having been thus murdered and sold, will not live again." And with those words he ushered Mr. Yeaman to the door and left him to supervise the loading of the Elephant's pelt on to a wagon. Upon his return to work a few moments later, Dr. Blair re-doubled his energies; he made no reference to his short disagreement with Mr. Yeaman; and I was wise enough not to make any mention of it.

We were soon made aware that the hind feet of an Elephant are much the same as the fore-feet. Only, there are two of them. The hind foot has a *Tarsus*, a number of bones forming the heel; and the foot is favoured with five toes, one less than the number on the fore-foot. One must suppose that the addition of the *Tarsus* and the smaller number of toes, along with the double bones of *Tibia* and *Fibula*, are designed to assist in supporting the great weight of the rear parts of the Elephant. This struck me quite clearly as I made my drawings but I made no comment aloud: such secrets were now mine, not to be given to the anatomist.

Our study of the hind feet, interrupted as it was by the visit paid by Mr. Yeaman, took us all of the morning; we broke off from our task to have our dinner. Miss Gloag appeared from somewhere just at the opportune moment, and served me up – from a pot of bad grace – using a ladle of insults – into a bowl of indifference – some provocative stew – accompanied by several lumps of bread – leavened by the ferment of the most sinful language a man should ever have to hear: all of which, despite the manner in which it was offered, was excellent. After the meal, nodding my compliments to my disappointed audience of the constantly rotating kitchen-maid and the large black cat, I used the short interruption to our experiments to look in on my mother, who seemed to be pleased with her new surroundings.

"Aye, Gibby," said she, "you have done well at last. This is a fine house you have bought. Your father would have been right pleased."

I chose not to dispel her illusions as to the nature of our present accommodations; and left her engraving patterns in the dust and grime of the attic-room.

Dr. Blair being called away to saw the leg off a stone-mason's apprentice, I had an hour to myself to look over all my drawings from this day and the preceding days and put them in some order. I confess that I look forward with keen anticipation to the days when I will be my own mas-ter, ordered about by none, engraving my own drawings upon my own copper plates. Even if the plates were for the profit of another man, they would forever be my own engravings. Moments such as these, which are few in my life, are to be savoured for the promise of immortality[75] which they offer, for myself and for the Last Elephant.

In this hour of solitary contemplation I was inter-rupted by a great commotion in the kitchen below, as if a flock of geese, chased by several dogs, had burst in upon Miss Gloag. Startled by this, I hurried below stairs; and found that my own family had arrived for a visit. Of course, the noise came not from them; but from the usual gang of Hendrie's children who had chosen to ac-company my own ones here; while my wife and children

---

75. Ah, Mr. Orum: Immortality. You sought it at every turn, and at every turn it eluded you. Few indeed are those whose names are made immortal: the great Latin Poets, the Greek Philosophers, our Scotch Scientists and Economists and Churchmen, Sir Walter Scott – names we all know; but not that of Gilbert Orum. So much for Immortality.

made themselves very small in a corner, Miss Gloag laid about herself with oaths and kitchen implements, trying to quell the on-rushing horde. With only slightly more authority vested in my person than Miss Gloag, I managed to clear the whole tribe out into the yard, where they made sport with the fat cat, which had not the wit to hide; the kitchen-maid all-twirling; and a wheelbarrow; while I talked briefly to my family, who soon, however, profited from the distraction of their cousins to slip away.

Shortly afterwards, at around two o'clock, Dr. Blair returned from his appointment with the mason's apprentice; remaining utterly calm in the face of the imminent destruction of his home and property, he gathered Hendrie's brood around him; then pulled from a bloody cloth the severed leg, whose recent history he proceeded to relate to them; re-enacting, with his soiled instruments, the amputation. The instant effect of this educative tale upon Hendrie's children was most productive, as they turned white with fear, and fled screaming into the street.[76]

I watched with growing unease, as the doctor placed the leg in a tub of spirits; washed the blood from his hands at the pump; then, without further ado, summoned us to the task. Mr. Menteith, who had in Mr. Butler's absence on a visit to Meigle accompanied the surgeon on his recent expedition, looked greatly invigorated by this experience, and was even less restrained in his objectionable enthusiasms than heretofore.

There can be nothing more wearisome for an engraver than the *Vertebrae* of any animal; for these bones,

---

76. Education; education; education. Dr. Blair was quite correct.

being large in number and very similar in appearance, have no great interest; once one has drawn one *Vertebra*, one has almost drawn all the *Vertebrae* of the world. I say this in despite of Dr. Blair's assertions to the contrary. The neck has seven of these bones, and the spine a further nineteen of them; were one to narrow one's eyes and observe all of these bones, one would say that they are identical. It is in the nature of philosophers, however, to distinguish the smallest Difference in everything that to any sane man might be the same; and to worry at these small differences; and to philosophize around them, in order to prove that the philosopher's philosophy is far more meticulous than his neighbour's. It is the nature of a craftsman, on the contrary, to show in his work the common Unity of all things.

Miss Gloag's excellent stew began to take its toll upon my concentration; my eye-lids frequently drooped and the pen dropped silently from my hands. At such moments, the weight of my head as it fell towards my chest pulled me rudely back into wakefulness, just in time to avoid the attention of the surgeon. Mr. Menteith, alas, noticed my tiredness, and offered up exaggerated and doubtless witty representations of my lethargy. I was therefore pleased that we moved along the nineteen *Vertebrae* of the spine in some haste, noting and measuring in size and weight the pairs of ribs which are suspended from each.

"The spine," observed Dr. Blair, "is perhaps the most important set of bones in any of God's creatures which walks upon the land, for it offers all the strength to support the head and the entire weight of the body. Without a spine, indeed, none of us would be able to move about, nor hold our head high and consider the glories of the Wise Creator's works. We may not," he added bleakly, "say the same of the Commissioners now meeting in Edinburgh, who appear to function perfectly well without a spine."[77]

Finally, we came to the tail, which consisted of no fewer than nine-and-twenty *Vertebrae*, each succeeding one being smaller than its neighbour. We affected no surprise at this diminution. Dr. Blair was in grand philosophical mood, and alerted us, as we prepared to put away for the evening our instruments and papers, to a co-incidence with the number of Commissioners for Scotland; "These gentleman number one-and-thirty," he pronounced, "there are among them perhaps two who do not intend to sell the future of Scotland for their own profit. This leaves us with nine-and-twenty, who form the tail that is being shaken by the Queen of England and her powerful Lords. My friends," he said to us, calling our attention to his heavy wit and doubtful arithmetic, "how much, I wonder, does our Elephant illustrate for us the perilous state of our country!"

I began, rather, to wonder about my supper.[78]

---

77. Dr. Blair unfortunately repeats some of the unfounded assertions of Lockhart and Fletcher; he was not to know just how matters proceeded in Edinburgh, as we – with the benefit of hindsight – do. The Act of Union of 1707 was the bed-rock, the very fundament of Great Britain's rise to pre-eminence as a Land of Enterprise, Science, Literature and Tartan. Without the glorious Union, Scotchmen would never have pulled themselves from the mires of Darien and Jacobitism, nor found their voice upon the Stage of History. So much for Invertebrates.

78. Who, but an unschooled charlatan, would prefer his Supper

Having delivered these full and exact descriptions of the Lords in Edinburgh, Dr. Blair instructed us to attend on the following day, so that we might complete our meas' urement of the dimensions and weights of all the bones which we possessed.

When supper was completed, I made my excuses to my mother and went out into the town. Miss Gloag, anxious, no doubt, to be rid of unwelcome guests, had advised me that there was a room available for rent in the house of Mr. Grant the baker. I, too, was concerned not to impose upon Dr. Blair's hospitality for much longer; I knew I had to regain my family before another day passed, else they would find a home only under the stones in the kirk'yard; as for my mother, she had already begun to re' gard the huge house as her own domain, and the longer we stayed, the more difficult it would be to remove her, without the use of sharpened surgical tools; I did not wish to have such a great debt of gratitude to Dr. Blair that I would be unable to resist such changes as he frequently imposed upon my drawings; and finally, for every day that I stayed, it was certain that I would be paid less for my work.

In some agitation of spirit, then, I left the house of Dr. Blair, and made my way to the Cowgate, where Mr. Grant had his bakery. The shop had remained open late, to per' mit the God'fearing people of Dundee to purchase their bread for the Sabbath day. The baker, large and red, stood at his counter, smiling benignly upon his customers; his wife dispensed gossip and moral judgements; both man

---

before a Political Debate? We may judge Mr. Orum on this foolish absurdity alone.

and wife heaped abuse upon an aged assistant, who crept back and forth with loaves. When my turn came, I made my application to Mr. Grant; regally, he referred me to his wife; she, in turn, winked heavily at me, and asked me to wait a few minutes – the shop would shortly be closing, she would then attend to my needs.

After a good ten minutes, during which the final throng of customers arrived and left, and the chink of coins in Mr. Grant's drawer grew duller as the pile increased in size, Mr. Grant closed up his shop, whistled for a rather unpleasant dog, which growled at me by way of greeting, and announced that he was off down to the Nethergate for some fresh air.

"Mr. Grant likes to drink his fresh air," Mrs. Grant advised me, as she seized my arm with considerable force, and pulled me into the back of the shop. The lame assistant was wielding a broom that was at least twice his weight; he was dismissed with a cuff to the back of the head; whereupon he disappeared through the narrowest of doors into some unseen kennel.

"So, Mr. Orum," said Mrs. Grant, leaning forwards towards me that I might have a good view of her ample bosom, "you wish to rent my room?"

"Indeed," I replied, averting my gaze politely; I explained my situation as best I could.

"Oh, you poor man!" exclaimed Mrs. Grant as I told of the fire and its destructive consequences. "You poor, poor man!" She patted my person in an uncommonly intimate manner. "But surely the organs are not burnt?"

Adjusting my coat as decorously as I could to avoid her shameless investigation, I confirmed that I had not been harmed in any way at all. But that my night-shirt had turned to ashes – I should not have told her that, I suppose.

"A man who has gone through such a terrible, terrible shock must surely need some comfort, Mr. Orum?" The baker's wife prepared herself to give me as much comforting as I might desire. Such thoughts were, however, not uppermost in my mind. I cautioned the lady that her husband might at any time return from taking the air.

"We will not see Mr. Grant for several hours," said his wife derisively. "He likes to take very large draughts of fresh air. Come, Mr. Orum, let us see what we can do for you."

In some desperation, I tried to return the discussion to the matter of the room. She, however, dismissed this as being of no consequence – "The room is as good as yours, Mr. Orum," she hinted, "as long as you just put your mind at rest. Let us agree terms."

Alas, I am sad to say that I was obliged to put my mind at rest for several minutes while Mrs. Grant outlined to me, upon the kitchen-table, the terms of renting the room. Breathless at last, she then turned her attention to the matter of furniture for the room.

"All my furniture, I fear, was destroyed in the fire," I confessed.

"Well, well, well," said the lady, "I am sure I can provide you with some items – a table, a bed or two. I have, in addition, a rather comfortable seat. Have I not, Mr. Orum?"

As I gave consideration to the seat in question, my attention wandered a little; something curious caught my eye.

"Oh!" I exclaimed.

"Oh, indeed, Mr. Orum: oh!" she replied agreeably.

"No, Mrs. Grant, no!"

"Yes, Mr. Orum!" she contradicted encouragingly.

After a few moments, the misunderstanding was resolved. I indicated the item which had caught my attention: in a corner of the bakery, upon a bench next to the always-hot oven, was a very large piece of dough, visibly rising in the warmth. The shape of this grand loaf was uncannily like that of the left fore-foot of the Elephant; each time I looked at it, my conviction that it was that missing item perfectly increased.

I dared to ask Mrs. Grant about it.

"That, Mr. Orum," she said pleasantly, straightening her apron and powdering her damp forehead with flour, "is a special order that my husband has been asked to make up. It is rather fine, is it not?"

I conceded that it seemed considerably larger than the usual loaf.

"Indeed, Mr. Grant is not certain how the dough will rise, nor how the loaf will bake. But he has high hopes of a success."

"But," I ventured, "is it not the –?"

"Mr. Orum, you may be assured that it is precisely what you think it is. A certain important gentleman in this town has ordered the delicacy, as he has arranged a political supper for Monday night, and wishes to have a grand and unusual centre-piece for the feast."

"And that gentleman is –?"

Mrs. Grant wagged her finger at me and simpered grossly. "Oh, Mr. Orum, a lady is not at liberty to give away such secrets. Unless, of course, a gentleman wishes to extract her secrets by brute force?" I preferred not to pursue the matter to its improper conclusion. I could guess who the 'important gentleman' might be.

I tried another approach. "That item," I said, adopting a grave tone, and brushing copious amounts of flour from my clothes, "is the property of my patron, Dr. Blair. It should, in all legality, be returned to him forthwith."

Mrs. Grant looked at me with disappointment in her face, gathering a shawl over her bosom. "I think," she said with some coolness, "that if our agreement on the room is to stand, Mr. Orum, then the item must stay here."

I understood her. There was no need to weigh the moral arguments against the practical ones. I sighed. The good lady dusted me down some more, and then, repent-ing of her scolding, revealed her secret of how the item had come to the bakery. It had, it seemed, been brought by the 'important political gentleman' late on Wednesday evening last; the gentleman had revealed that it had been presented to him by Mr. Campbell, the fish-monger (at this disclosure, I gasped in horror at the duplicity of the man), in expectation of future custom. Mr. Campbell had, in turn, alleged that he himself had received it from Mr. Alexander Blair on the previous evening, in exchange for fresh fish – again, I was not able to contain my expres-sions of disappointment; Mr. Blair, for his part, advised Mr. Campbell that the foot had been surrendered to him by a notorious highwayman and robber, who much frequented the road to Perth, and who had robbed 'two foreign Johnnies' of this prize; on being captured, the highway-man – known commonly as '*Kilspindie Blether-Shanks*'[79] for his propensity to be distracted by gossip dur-ing the exercise of his craft – had offered the item to Mr. Blair, in an attempt to avoid the scaffold.

All of these revelations almost unmanned me; my knees trembled; Mrs. Grant offered me her seat; I took it distractedly; I was restored to equilibrium; we agreed at last on terms for the room. I hastened to tell my family the good news; my wife sobbed uncontrollably and my children screamed and wept: we are again happy.

I sit this night in Dr. Blair's house, writing in my Journal, knowing that at last my tribulations will soon be at an end. Despite which comforting knowledge, I can-not sleep.

---

79. We have found but one mention of this Highwayman in the magistrates' records for Dundee: he was alleged to be the junior partner of the infamous *Inchyra Irritater*, whose dastardly attacks upon the coach between Perth and Dundee excited wrath and despondency in equal proportion. The *Irritater* was never apprehended, and *Kilspindie Blether-shanks* escaped the gibbet only because he produced two witnesses, one a minister of the Kirk, who could place him ten miles away at the time of the crime of which he was accused. So much for Justice.

16 JUNE 1706.

Since my family moved in to the room provided by Mrs. Grant, I have neglected my journal.[80] There are many reasons for this, but the most pressing one is the need to hide from everyone, not least myself, the conditions under which I am obliged to pay rent. What if I were to write something of the matter in my journal, and my wife, or my mother, or – worse – my dear little Agnes, were to find it? Dr. Blair, ever one to instruct, had read to Mr. Menteith, in my hearing, a passage in a book by Monsieur Tavernier, on Elephants: "The Female makes her bed some four or five feet high from the ground, where she throws herself, and lies on her back in expectation of the male, whom she invites by a peculiar cry."[81] Mr. Menteith leered at me on hearing these words: I suspect that he knows of my unwilling agreement with Mrs. Grant. All I can suppose is that Mr. Tavernier, perhaps an honest craftsman like myself, had had difficulties in paying his rent.

In the second half of the month of May, the weather in Dundee continued to be hot and dry; fortunately, no

---

80. We consider this neglect unforgivable. A man who writes a Journal should not let his responsibility slide. There can be no excuse. How is *History* ever to be recorded, when once *Holidays*, *Idleness* and *Carelessness* creep in?

81. This remark by M. Tavernier, who was clearly a Frenchman, may have been put up by Dr. Blair in his Essay, but only so that Dr. Blair could knock it down again. Mr. Orum has no business with it, using it as a tattered fig-leaf to cover his monstrous lewdness.

longer did I have to spend those hot days in close proximity to the decaying flesh and desiccated inner parts of the
Last Elephant.

I was not idle: I had my drawings to finish, and then
I had need to start in upon the work of engraving. Dr.
Blair demanded – doubtless so that he would dictate to
me what I should draw – that I carry out some of this
work in his study, a grand room over-looking the River
Tay, with a view to the distant hills and woods of the
Kingdom of Fife beyond; in the afternoon, after another
good dinner from Miss Gloag, I would find myself slumbering, my eye-lids closing in the heavy warm air. This
was no great surprise, as I sleep little at night: my mother
continues to cry out, and I fear her howling will exhaust
the patience of our landlady; Mr. Grant and his apprentices rattle about underneath us in the bakery from the
earliest hours; his unpleasant dog growls incessantly at
our door, doubtless excited by the heavy smell of the Last
Elephant slumbering within; and I am always in dread
of Mrs. Grant approaching by stealth and by darkness,
to remind me of my obligations. When I sleep, I sleep
with one eye and one ear open. I awake before dawn and
lament my situation; I worry for my family, whose spirits had been broken by the fire and their stay with their
cousins; I lie awake, convinced that we will never find a
home again; I lie awake and curse myself for my greed
in my contract with Mr. Sutherland; I am troubled that
the missing fore-foot has not yet re-appeared, and that my
part in its disappearance will be discovered. I am torment-
ed by this thought: if indeed '*Kilspindie Blether-Shanks*'
really exists, then it can not be long before he comes to
hear how his reputation has been abused and chooses to

deny any part in the matter. An untruth, once snagged, will soon unravel.

Dr. Blair was not idle: having expended so much time and energy since the last days of April, in capturing, flaying, dissecting and enumerating the parts of the Elephant; he found that he had let slide some of his duties as a surgeon, and as an apothecary, and as a teacher, and as a botanist. With enthusiasm re-doubled, therefore, he flung himself back into those affairs from dawn until dusk. He was scarcely ever in the house; appearing only for his dinner; then returning again in the evening, just as I completed my duties. Our meetings were necessarily short – a fact which was profoundly pleasing to me, since it meant that he did not have the time to interfere in my preparation of the drawings or engravings. While he busied himself thus, his wife Elizabeth came to full term and gave birth, late in the month of May, to another boy. Dr. Blair was much affected by this event; so was Miss Gloag who cursed vehemently, then shed tears.

Neither had Mr. Yeaman been idle: on the eighth day of June, a Saturday, he became the Provost of the town of Dundee, by a large majority amongst the gentlemen voters. Mr. Alexander Blair was outraged. But Mr. Yeaman had, it seemed, cultivated his voters by means of flattery, small presents, political suppers and cups of tea; had one by one brought them within his circle and charmed them; as they succumbed to such bribes, Mr. Blair's party had one by one cast them off as lost friends and treacherous acquaintances, and did not shirk from the duty of telling these apostates of their worst faults. It fell to Mr. Yeaman, in his lengthy speech of victory, which he delivered to the assembled crowds from the window of the town-hall, to announce also a great victory by the English General Wellington, over the French, at some place named '*Ramlays*'. Mr. Yeaman was careful not to suggest that the victory had fallen to 'Great-Britain', or to 'our Queen'; for he was not unaware of the strong feelings in the town on the matter of the Treaty of Union. But he did suggest, in religious manner, that God was a speaker of English, and not of Dutch, French or Spanish. The very mention of the Dutch and Spaniards brought a great hissing and booing from the crowd, who execrated those perfidious fishers upon the seas.[82]

Mr. Yeaman continued not to be idle: he had a far greater ambition than merely becoming Provost of Dundee. He had hopes to sit in Parliament. To that end, he organized a most lavish supper for all his friends. This supper took place last night. I will profitably pass this Sabbath day in describing the event.

Almost everyone who had any standing in Dundee attended the Grand Victory Supper in the town-hall, a week after the Provost's election: masters of the spinning and weaving trades; farmers of substance; captains of merchant-ships; surgeons; lawyers; tradesmen of wealth. Those who were not invited, nor felt that they should have been, turned up in great numbers outside the town-hall: to insult the guests as they arrived; to cluster round

82. We are, we suppose, grateful to Mr. Orum for his reports of Mr. Yeaman's championing of the cause of *Great Britain* among a doubtful citizenry. These past 120 years have shown, time and again, that Mr. Yeaman had great foresight.

the windows to hear all the speeches; to gaze in stupefac-
tion upon the supper laid out within. Those who were
not invited, but felt that they should have been, stayed
away; and burned alone in miserable covetousness. Some
attended a rival supper on the preceding evening, hosted
by Alexander Blair, a bitter and silent affair; Mrs. Grant
advises me in confidence that several of that party fell vio-
lently ill at the table, from the consumption of a pudding
made of brains in brandy.

It was my good fortune to attend the Grand Victory
Supper; not as one invited by virtue of wealth and standing; but as one who would record the scene for posterity.
I was permitted a small stool in a dark corner at the back
of the hall, from which perch, like an owl, I could gaze out
upon the riot before me. It goes without saying that no
ladies were permitted to attend this feast; for, were they
truly ladies, they would not have endured more than ten
minutes of the carousing company of the great and the
good of Dundee.[83]

I shall not record here any detail of what occurred
that evening. If a man has ever witnessed dissipation,
abandonment, excess, indulgence, profligacy, waste; if a
man has seen others slip down beneath a swirling tide
of ale and spirits; if a man has stood appalled while large
plates of food were over-turned intemperately and cast
vulgarly to the floor; if a man has listened aghast at the
foulest of language and the loosest of talk; if a man has

---

83. Ladies have, of course, no business being present at any such
suppers, either in 1706 or in 1830. Their place is in the home, as
Mrs. S. always said. A lady who attends such a supper is no lady at
all. We have attended such a Supper at which a Female was present.

cried in despair at the baseness of the human spirit; then a man might readily imagine the rout. The watchers at the windows did not lack amusement, nor will they lack the opportunity in the coming days and weeks to entertain their fellows with tales of turpitude.

At the mid-point of the evening, when a peak of hilarity and rude cheerfulness had been attained; and just before the assembled worthies lost all understanding of their surroundings; Mr. Yeaman called for silence in order to make yet another speech. Already that evening, in the space of two hours, he had made seven speeches of one sort and another – thanking this group of people, bestowing gratitude upon that, toasting Queen Anne with one hand and 'the distressed royal family' of James with the other; celebrating the Commissioners of Scotland and England alike; decrying the loss of Scotland's honour in Darien; praising both the Duke of Hamilton and the Earl of Stair; in short, being a good friend to all men, and celebrating them all in one embrace. Now, he called for some silence; and asked Dr. Patrick Blair to rise from his seat.

Dr. Blair, being a man who knew the most intimate secrets of every man in the room, and of every man's wife, was loudly applauded and long. He stood, smiling gravely and bowing in all directions, then turned an inquiring look upon Mr. Yeaman.

"My friends," began Mr. Yeaman, "have we not all admired Dr. Patrick Blair's great mind over the years that he has been with us here in the thriving town of Dundee?" Many agreed that they had spent their days and nights marvelling at the mind of Dr. Blair. "And have we not all – every man here – thanked him for relieving our pain and salving our sores?" Every man roared their conviction that, without Dr. Patrick Blair, they would not be alive to attend this supper tonight. "I, too, have good reason to thank our very good friend," Mr. Yeaman concurred; then paused, long enough for some more innocent souls in the throng to speculate whether Mr. Yeaman might be about to reveal the secret of a degenerate illness, or of some similar amatory indisposition. In which speculation they were soon disappointed.

"For it is Dr. Blair," he went on, calling for utter silence, "who, with all his skill and knowledge, has so recently taken the sad corpse of my Elephant, and preserved it for the greater honour of Dundee, for the perpetual association of the name of our town with that of Enlightenment and Discovery,[84] and who will shortly re-generate that Elephant for all time!"

At this announcement, wild applause burst out, accompanied by looks of considerable incomprehension.

When the noise had died down again, Mr. Yeaman continued: "Ah, but I forget: Dr. Blair is missing one thing from our Elephant! Is that not the case, sir?"

Dr. Blair looked puzzled, then slowly nodded.

"If that be the case," announced the Provost smugly, "then look behind you!"

Dr. Blair turned round from his seat; then bent down and picked up some heavy object. During the preceding uproar, some servant of Mr. Yeaman had evidently crept round the back of the top table, and placed there

---

84. Indeed, he might have said that all of Scotland would shortly become associated with Enlightenment. But Mr. Yeaman did well to name *Dundee* as the town of *Discovery* – something our City Fathers might find it profitable to note.

– the missing left fore-foot of the Elephant! Dr. Blair was astounded and amazed. Mr. Yeaman was red and triumphant. The crowd was startled and gratified. I dropped my pens and paper, struck suddenly by remorse and a premonition of unwelcome revelation. Dr. Blair patted the item tenderly and nodded to Mr. Yeaman, who waved regally. Even from the great distance at which I sat, it was easy to observe that the foot had greatly suffered in its absence of six weeks: the flesh was dried and the muscles had shrunk to nothing, the bones were exposed and yellowed.

The whole thing was unaccountably encrusted in stale dough and crumbs. Dr. Blair stood up on the table to make a speech of thanks. He was constrained to wait for several minutes while the crowd replenished their glasses and toasted him.

"My good friends," he began, at which address, he was roundly toasted again. "My good friends, and Mr. Yeaman: I am most grateful to receive this final limb of the Elephant. It has been missing since that day at the end of April, when our beast died down by Broughty Ferry. I have no idea how Mr. Yeaman has come by the foot – " he looked at his host, who merely dismissed the question with a slight movement of his hand, the while smirking upon his nearest neighbours at the high table. " – but I am most glad that it has come back to me. It will, when it has been cleaned and boiled and entered into my Osteology, be a most handsome complement to the rest of the skeleton."

Plaudits resounded to the rafters; and several of the cloth-masters made a note to refer to their privies hereafter as 'The Osteology'.

"If I might be permitted, on this happy occasion, to make a small announcement?" Dr. Blair was permitted – not one man would have lived to see the morning had he gain-said the request.

"It is my intention to establish in our great and glorious town of Dundee" – loud cheers – "a grand Hall of Rarities, in which the most remarkable items of our town may be preserved and kept safe for our children and our grand-children and all their children, for years to come." While there were no cheers to greet this proposal, there was an unusual hum of intelligence and approbation. "Our Hall of Rarities will form an excellent companion to our famous Physic Garden; Dundee will become a centre of learning and philosophy. I will also inaugurate a 'Natural History Society', here in Dundee: it will be the envy of all Scotland." There was some polite applause at this, but most of the audience began to peer hopefully into their mugs; Physic Gardens and Halls of Rarities were not necessarily of consuming interest to the merchants and traders. Dr. Blair seemed to detect this shift of mood, for he then continued: "And into our Hall of Rarities I will place firstly our Elephant, which will stand in Death as it did in Life, and be a great wonder to behold." There were signs of grudging enthusiasm. "And I would hope," he added, "that the skeletons of other admirable Rarities will be displayed there in years to come – perhaps," he paused reflectively, "perhaps our very own Mr. George Yeaman, if he is elected to Parliament, might consider donating his bones to our Hall, after his death?"

A sudden silence descended on the crowd, broken only by appreciative shouts of support from those clinging to the window-sills. But it did not last long. Mr. George

Yeaman rose unsteadily from his throne, and raised a glass of port-wine.

"Dr. Blair," he called slowly, his voice slurred, doubtless by the emotion aroused, "Dr. Blair, you are a man of over-abundant wisdom and vision. Let me be the first, after my Elephant, to have my bones assembled and displayed in our Hall of Rarities. It would be for me a great honour to be exhibited, and a great honour for all my fellow-townsmen to have me there!"

It took several moments for the crowd to digest what had been said; to look askance; to consider whether Mr. Yeaman was in earnest; to decide that he was; and then to raise the roof in cheers of rapture. Dr. Blair looked greatly surprised, but said nothing further; and sat down once more, balancing the left fore-foot in his lap.

I JULY 1706.

In the past few days, since that Supper, men of wealth
have been arriving at Dr. Blair's house; they clutch bags
of silver which they wish to subscribe to the building of
the Hall of Rarities; each one is led into the study, where
I sit quietly at my work, and is permitted several minutes
of Dr. Blair's time. The amounts are written ceremoni-
ously into a ledger. The visitor's name is inscribed in
the 'Grand Roll of Members of the Society for Natural
Improvements of Dundee'. Then the trader or master or
merchant or lawyer will whisper something in Dr. Blair's
ear, and take his leave. Dr. Blair has, of course, not shared
with me any of this secretive conversation: but it is not
difficult to understand that each man of note in Dundee
wishes to have his bones repose in perpetuity in the 'Hall
of Rarities'.[85]

---

85. If the heroic Vikings of old lived with the promise of *Valhalla*
when they died, why should not our own heroes of Dundee live
likewise? A man would surely be proud to be displayed to the
admiring gaze of his fellow-citizens.

As a boy, we much frequented the 'Hall of Rarities' and can well
remember its contents; for, besides the great Elephantine remains,
which formed the centre-piece and greatest rarity, there were other
skeletons, both of the human and brute species, hung about the
walls. We can evidence the following exhibits and their adjoined
epitaphs:

Item, the skeleton of Provost R. "who always voted for an
independent member of Parliament, and was never known to have
lent his name to a borough job";

item, the skeleton of Bailie T. who had "graduated as an A.M. in the University of Edinburgh and possessed the address and manners of a gentleman";

item, the skeleton of Town-Counsellor O. "who, during the only year he was allowed to remain in office, voted in opposition to the chair";

item, the skeleton of Deacon D. who was "elected ten times to that distinguished office, and was never seen drunk on a Michaelmas-day";

item, the skeleton of Provost M. "who, during a long leadership of the Council, never trafficked with his colleagues in borough property";

item, the skeleton of Bailie C. who "quitted the Council-board because he was allowed to stand single in voting for a presentation to a parson who was anxiously wished and petitioned for by the Congregation";

item, the skeleton of Jeremy Turnkey who held the office of gaoler for twenty years, and "retained to the last the milk of human kindness – shedding tears for unfortunate debtors, and refusing in many cases to accept gaol fees";

item, the skeleton of Provost Y. who, "by a dexterous manoeuvre, obtained for himself the representation of the five boroughs in Parliament, and made a faithful use of the trust reposed in him";

item, the skeleton of Town-clerk S. who "peremptorily refused to accept an additional salary of a hundred pounds Scots, because the Council would not allow his colleague in office to participate in it".

Here, indeed, was a fine collection of the Great and the Worthy of Dundee! We regret that the practice of mounting for public approbation the bones of town dignitaries and Members of Parliament is no longer widespread. The abandonment of this custom is, we would argue, a very great loss to Christian Understanding, and to the Civic Education of Young People everywhere. Surely such a sobering and instructive practice needs be continued? We have more than once written a letter to the news-paper on this very matter; and should the honourable practice be adopted once again, we would only ask, out of charitable concern,

I am in some perplexity to understand whether Dr. Blair truly means to display the skeletons of these inspired men; or whether he hopes only to build his Hall with their money, and then let the feelings of widows and children stand in the way of any singular sepulchres. I can think of several men who have lately requested a permanent exhibition of their bones, who would be far better six feet below the cold, cold earth, bothering no one, reminding no one of their brief and bitter existence, of their unlamented demise. Perhaps that is uncharitable: we are all destined to die, and perhaps the 'Hall of Rarities' awaits us; and perhaps it does not; it is not for us to decide; but surely it is not for the chink of coins to decide.

I amuse myself with this thought: were all of these men of substance of a sudden to die – perhaps of the plague, or of over-indulgence in the broth of an Elephant at a political supper, or be cut down in civil disturbance and riot[86] – how then would we find a vat large enough to boil up all their bones and have them mounted for display? And how big would the 'Hall of Rarities' need to be to accommodate them?

---

that the gentlemen be allowed to die a natural death before being displayed in such a manner.

We believe that Dr. Blair's innovation has since been copied by a macabre French-woman, delighting in the name of Madame Tussocks, who has toured our island in recent years with a collection of corpses. They cannot compete with good British corpses. So much for France.

86. Mr. Orum 'amuses' himself with such horrible diversions! What manner of man is he? The Great Terror in France, now – thanks be to God – a distant nightmare, can have thrown up no worse examples of Devilry than Mr. Orum's notions.

22 JULY 1706.

It was on this day, the twenty-and-second of July in the
year 1706, that I have finally parted ways with Dr. Patrick
Blair, surgeon-apothecary of Dundee, and would-be
Fellow of the Royal Society. I am greatly pleased, yet my
hand trembles even as I consider what it is I have done.
For today, Dr. Blair has begun his task of assembling the
bones of the Last Elephant; and Mr. Orum has begun his
task of stuffing its skin. In a few months from now, there
will be two exhibits in the Dundee 'Hall of Rarities' – one
will be a motionless skeleton and the other will be the
Elephant as she was when last seen alive. We shall see
then which of us has served the Last Elephant best.[87]

87. We shall see, indeed, Mr. Orum! Indeed, let us not delay – we
shall see now: Mr. Orum slips swiftly into obscurity, with never a
penny to his name, nor a single engraving of any note displayed in
any house of respectability. On the other hand, the brief biographical
facts of Dr. Patrick Blair's further career are these: he finally
published his great Essay in the Philosophical Transactions of the
Royal Society of London, in the year 1710. So long and so diverting
was his Essay, that it was published in two parts – *Ars Longa, Vita
Brevis!* In the later part of that same year, Dr. Blair and his family
moved to the quiet town of Coupar Angus, leaving behind him his
Physic Garden and his Hall of Rarities. He received an honour from
the University of Aberdeen, in the year 1712; in that same year,
he became a 'Fellow of the Royal Society'; in 1713, he travelled to
London to see Sir Hans Sloane and other new friends, and made a
visit to Oxford to view the Physic Garden there; before returning by
Lichfield and Birmingham. And then came the unfortunate events of
1715, when he abandoned Coupar Angus and his young family, and
threw in his lot with Lord Nairn's battalion in the armies of James

the Pretender, only to be captured at Preston, and to be dragged in ignominy to London.

At his trial, on March 31st, 1716, at which he pleaded guilty with his fellow-prisoners to the charge of taking up arms against the Government and Throne of Great Britain, Dr. Blair was sentenced to death. Thanks in part to the concerned intervention of Dr. Hans Sloane of the Royal Society, but also to the Natural Mercy and Innate Goodness of our Monarchy, he was granted a reprieve at the eleventh hour, and was released from Newgate Prison, penniless, homeless; but – a simple blessing to which we might all aspire – not friendless. Before long, he had resumed his botanical and philosophical investigations, and read several fascinating papers before the Royal Society, amongst which was a famous 'Discourse on the Sexes of Plants'; while, in 1719, an Addendum to his great Essay on the Elephant appeared in the Transactions of the Royal Society, having as its subject no less than 'The Organ of Hearing in the Elephant, with the Figures and Situation of the Ossicles, Labyrinth and Cochlea in the Ear of that large Animal.'

In April of 1720, he removed from London to the town of Boston in Lincolnshire, where he lived in quiet retreat until his death. From this tranquil spot, he worked on and issued in sections his greatest work, the *Pharmaco-Botanologia, an Alphabetical and Classical Dissertation on all the British Indigenous and Garden Plants of the New London Dispensatory*, a grand labour from which he was called away – peremptorily – by Death himself, in February 1728, having advanced only as far as the letter 'H'. It is thought that Dr. Blair, FRS, was in his fifty-third year when he died. But let us, if our Readers will indulge us, bring Dr. Blair's own words into this all-too-brief Footnote – these are his high-soaring thoughts from the Preface to his *Pharmaco-Botanologia*:

"Being obliged to give Botanical Lectures at Dundee to some Students in Physic and Pharmacy, then under my Care, I first planted the Dispensatory Plants alphabetically in my Garden, and then dictated a History of them in Latin […] Now being retired to a Country Place, I have proposed to employ my leisure Hours in

discoursing on the Practical, as I formerly did on the Theoretical
part of the Indigenous and Home-bred Vegetables […] Yet, not to
withdraw myself from the Exercise of my Profession in too close a
Pursuit of a prolix Subject, I propose to parcel out a few Plants at
a time to give the Reader time to Ruminate upon one Part while
I am preparing another for his Entertainment […] My reader will
soon see no ostentatious Affectation, no vainglorious Itching to
be an Author, has prompted me to publish a Work upon a Subject
of this Nature; I plead not the Desire and Solicitations of Friends;
what I have most in my View, is, to manifest the Glory of God
and his Omnipotence in endowing Man with a rational Faculty
to discern these wonderful Productions of his divine Wisdom,
and his providential Care over Man; who, as he has since the Fall
been liable to such Infirmities as the Weakness of his Nature, the
Mismanagement of himself in this lapsed State, or perhaps various
Inclinations or his immoderate Debaucheries have brought upon
him, and made him subject to divers Diseases, and various Tortures,
Torments, and bodily Pains and Afflictions; so he has provided such
a vast Variety of Remedies […]"

Ah! – "no vainglorious Itching to be an Author" : would that more
men – and now, we understand, certain incautious ladies – took
these words into their hearts and there examined them well in an
hour of sobriety: would not the world be a more regulated place?
Contrast Dr. Blair's elevated thoughts, with those mean ones of Mr.
Orum!

   Thus did Dr. Blair dedicate his life to the pursuit of *Botanical*,
Anatomical and *Philosophical* knowledge, for the greater benefit of
his fellow-creatures, weak and pitiful though we are. For our part,
we have always taken of the wormwood (as Dr. Blair many times
proposed) for the treatment of any agues and fevers; a marvellous
remedy of Nature which we would recommend to all Editors. The
work of Surgeon Blair, and that of his fellows, opened up the vast
museum of the natural world to all of us, one since classified by the
Swedish scholar Linnaeus. Thus did Dr. Blair serve Science and the
Elephant.

This is how I parted from Dr. Blair: when all the names of gentleman subscribers to the 'Hall of Rarities' and the 'Natural History Society' had been gathered, which did not take more than a week, Dr. Blair sought out a suitable building for the Hall; it would not be possible, he said, for him to mount the skeleton in one house and hope to trans- port it intact to another. The search did not meet with many obstacles since each and every man of substance in Dundee, who owned any building larger than a bothy, offered Dr. Blair some share of his premises; the unspo- ken payment demanded was that of being mounted, at a future date, for immortality. After inspecting several promising edifices, Dr. Blair decided upon a building that had once been a store for turnips. It was high, airy, and the ground was level – a feature most unusual in the buildings of Dundee. Light and fresh breezes were admit- ted through high windows; the roof did not leak during the summer rains. All of which qualified it as a building that was more sound than most homes in the town; and such was to be the new home of *Florentia*, now dead, but hereafter enjoying a life and house that could be the envy of every weaver, spinner, fisher, labourer and engraver.

On twenty-second day of July,[88] all of the bones – including those of the re-united left fore-foot of the Elephant, now cleansed and dried with all of its fellows – were loaded carefully into a pair of carts and transported at a funereal and graceful pace to the new Hall of Rarities.

---

88. In a continuation of that strange series of co-incidences, the 22nd of July 1706 was the very day that the Commissioners reached agreement on the twenty-five Articles of the 'Union of the Kingdoms of Scotland and England'.

Some workmen were within, completing various minor repairs to the building (all at the expense of Mr. William Duncan, the well-known turnip-merchant). We entered: the building was truly a splendid setting; the floor was laid in brick, and the sun warmed the air. Dr. Blair rubbed his hands: "I think," he said to the world in general, "we will find ourselves most comfortable here. Let us begin."

At that very moment, fearing no doubt that his influ-ence over the affairs of Dundee might be dimmed by Dr. Blair's proposed labours, Mr. George Yeaman arrived. Behind him, struggling with a hand-cart of such propor-tions that I suppose it must have been built solely for its present purpose, came my brother Hendrie and his friend Mr. Fairweather: in the hand-cart was a shapeless pile of rough grey objects soon recognized as the bristly pelt of the Last Elephant.

"Dr. Blair," shouted Mr. Yeaman, panting for breath, "not so fast!"

Dr. Blair nodded politely in greeting, and waited while Mr. Yeaman recovered himself, the hill from the town-house being rather steep. Hendrie and Watty took the opportunity to lean on the long handles of their barrow.

"I have here," continued Mr. Yeaman, again the master of his lungs, "the pelt of my Elephant, which I gladly yield up to the towns-people of Dundee. It shall," he announced to the throng which now surrounded us – the establishment of a 'Hall of Rarities' being a marvel in Dundee, the crowd consisted of five old men, a cluster of women on their way back from the fish-market, three boys and a hen – "It shall stand alongside our skeleton within this memorable building." With these words, he raised his arms to encompass the full height and width of the turnip-store. One of the old men raised a hoarse cheer; his four comrades denounced him. The hen fluttered onto the barrow and began to peck about with great interest.

Dr. Blair was clearly not pleased with this announce-ment, but was unable to gainsay it. "Of course," he said, "the Elephant must be presented in both its philosophical guise and its outward appearance. I welcome your kind offer, sir." Like two fist-fighters about to knock out each other's teeth, they shook hands. "And who," asked Dr. Blair, "will stuff the skin for you?"

"My men here," replied Mr. Yeaman carelessly, in-dicating my brother and Watty. From their startled react-ion, this was manifestly a great surprise to both of them. Dr. Blair was astonished to an equal degree.

"But what do they know of stuffing a pelt?" he asked.

"That is no concern of yours, Dr. Blair," said Mr. Yeaman in lofty manner. "Let my men do their job, and you shall do yours. And Mr. Orum here -" he placed his hand in patronising manner upon my shoulder, "shall as-sist us. You, sir," he said to me in a tone that allowed of no denial, "will be pleased to direct your brother and his friend in their labours, will you not? There will be good money in it for you."

I stood for several moments. The attention of the world was upon me. I could refuse Mr. Yeaman's offer, and assist Dr. Blair in his scheme; or I could grasp this op-portunity to bring the Last Elephant to life, and preserve it for posterity. My moment had come – I had, after all, made my drawings and had begun on some of the engrav-ings: there was no other man in Dundee who could do that; but I was not willing to become a mere day-labourer for Dr. Blair in the matter of mounting the skeleton.[89]

Dr. Blair was, from that instant, my sworn enemy. His plans for the mounting of the skeleton had involved Mr. Menteith and myself, and – I now suppose – also my brother. Now, two of his company had gone over to the opposing army. He would have to re-group. He did so with remarkable ease: from every crevice and close in Dundee, surgeons and would-be philosophers reported for duty within the hour, all anxious to mount the Elephant.

The mounting of the Elephant: I should make it clear that this procedure does not involve a man climbing upon the back of an Elephant; nor indeed do we wish to repeat the coarse interpretation of Mr. Menteith; I use the word in its meaning of mounting the Elephant upon something else. At its simplest, this is the mounting of the Elephant upon the floor, so that it may stand as if it were alive – alive in all detail except, that is, for the lack of skin and movement, flesh and muscle, viscera and breath: that is, dead.

And the more honourable task of filling out the skin, of making the Elephant seem to live and breathe again, as she once had done, falls to Gilbert and Hendrie Orum. I sit here in the darkness, still shaking with awe at the momentous responsibility that now sits upon me.

---

89. If we had not been dealing with Mr. Gilbert Orum, we might feel some sympathy for a man put in the position of trying to serve two masters – the one Philosophical, the other Civic. But Mr. Orum's loyalties should have been clear. And where is the stuffed Elephant now, we ask? And where the magisterial Essay of Dr. Blair? So much for Posterity.

28 JULY 1706.

A week has passed since we began our long work. It does not go well. I knew that my brother had some skills, of which I had rarely wished to learn more, for they seemed to border upon the illegitimate. Watty Fairweather, however, has no skills to speak of, but made up for that in his enthusiasms for Hendrie's 'scrapes'. On our first day, I asked Hendrie: "Have you ever stuffed anything before?" Mr. Yeaman's champion denied this, although he remarked eagerly that he had once seen 'a stuffed trout in a man's house'. This was of little assistance to us. How Hendrie had persuaded Mr. Yeaman of his suitability for the job – I dared not ask. The Provost had, without doubt, other matters on his mind; we would have to make shift as best we could.

On the second day of last week, Dr. Blair was called away to a grand house out near Forfar, where his skills were urgently required in a matter of some discretion. I seized the opportunity of his absence, and the authority vested in me as the engraver, to visit Dr. Blair's study. Amongst all of his books I would surely find one that would show how a skin is stuffed. For three hours I searched, in constant fear that Dr. Blair would return, or that Mrs. Blair or the man Menteith would burst in upon me. At last, my nerves could take no more. I escaped from the house clutching two books, one containing the image of an Elephant, the other containing a passage on how a rodent was stuffed in Bristol in 1683.[90] I examined

---

90. This is, of course, the work by Mr. Howard, 'Concerning the Plague of Rodents in the Town of Bristol in the Year 1683, with Some Practical Advice on the Stuffing of Mouse-Skins; Compleat

these two books in every detail, copied the drawings and figures, and tried to understand the method of stuffing. The books were returned to Dr. Blair's study before he himself could notice their absence.

Yesterday, we were at last ready to begin our work, and my apprentices set to with praiseworthy energy. We acquired, through the orders of the Provost, some sacks of sawdust and bales of coarse unwashed wool. Large needles and thick thread were also in evidence: it was clear that Mr. Yeaman had, in his new mastery of Dundee, all the resources of a quarter-master. For hours on end, the huge grey skin heaved up and down under the assault of Hendrie and Watty.

But this evening, as we sat and gazed upon our work, we were in despair. "Gibby," said Hendrie wearily, "yon thing is just a big saft pillow." In truth, my brother was not mistaken: the head had been so badly stuffed and was so mis-shapen, that it resembled closely a huge leather ball, such as young men fight over at their annual matches; only the *Proboscis* dangled limply, for it had been so neglected in the matter of stuffing, that it hung down like an empty stocking. Watty remarked in a distracted manner that he had once seen Mr. Yeaman in undress.

I noticed Dr. Blair and Mr. Menteith standing at the other end of the Hall, where their pile of bones seemed slowly to grow into something with form; they pointed at us and I heard Menteith laugh.

What have I done?[91]

___

with Seven Illustrative Panels', which will be familiar to all of us.

91. What have you done, Sir? You have bitten off more than you can chew, Sir. You have taken the road of Pride and fallen in the ditch of Ignominy, Sir. We have seen such arrogance before, Sir.

18 AUGUST 1706.

At last – I believe that we have uncovered the secret of stuffing an Elephant!

Watty Fairweather surprised us all by discovering the trick. I had gone for a walk to clear my head; for three weeks we have been struggling with the pelt. Easier by far would it have been to pin a flying feather to a bluebottle. Meanwhile, at the farther end of the Hall, Dr. Blair's bones were rising from the ground, like an unearthly ghost – dead, but at least erect. As I returned from the harbour, where I had idly contemplated escape on a rotten ship bound for Denmark, I heard a shout and running footsteps; Hendrie had come looking for me. He dragged me back to the Hall, where, to my astonishment, I beheld a most lively object. Watty, with idle hands, had started to toy with the skin which had once clad the right fore-foot of the Elephant. With some pieces of wood which were lying nearby, and three short pieces of iron – both of which had been cast away by Dr. Blair's faction as they busied themselves with their skeleton – and with some wool and sawdust, Watty had soon put together a foot that was no mere cushion. Hendrie expressed our wonder: "Aye, if yon fit had but a road, it wid gang grand, eh?"

We will work with iron and wood, with wool and sawdust; starting with the head – whose stuffing is easily removed – and the trunk, then moving on to the body and the legs. A firm structure will be provided by iron – in the legs and to replace the *Vertebrae* – and pieces of wood will be readily shaped to represent the form of the Elephant; then each part of this structure will be inspected thoroughly by myself; should it fail to reach my high standards, the work will be taken apart and we will start again. At last, we all seem to know what we are doing, and the work is progressing well; Watty cuts the metal and the wood, according to command; and soaks the skin to make it pliable; and oils the skin to remove the scabs; and blisters his hands with the needles; Hendrie and I shape the iron, join the wood, and then cover the frame-work with the tough skin; when all is ready, Hendrie and Watty set to with a vengeance, packing the container thus formed with sawdust and wool as tightly as they can manage. We have today stuffed one foot and the trunk. At the far end of the Hall, the mockery of Mr. Menteith is silenced.

The Last Elephant will live again.[92]

---

92. We should not be surprised to learn that Dr. Blair has little to say concerning the stuffing of the skin. To be sure, he praises the result as "done to so good purpose and so lively"; but that is all that he chooses to say. For Dr. Blair, as for all discerning Readers, the Skeleton was the thing, not some wayward whim of an unskilled engraver, his rascally brother and an Idiot. Mr. Orum has talked of 'idle hands' – we need not remind ourselves what the Devil does with idle hands.

By contrast, let us examine the method by which Dr. Blair proceeded, a method which he describes closely, over eight pages, in his Essay:

"I come now to the last thing I propos'd, which is the Method I us'd in mounting the Sceleton; and because Dr. Moulins's way of nailing a Plate of Iron to the Roof of the Mouth, in which the Iron Rod that runs through the Vertebrae of the Neck was fast'ned, would have been inconvenient, by spoiling the back-part of the Scull, obstructing its View, and making the Head look too much forward, which was the fault of his Sceleton, I contriv'd another, which is as follows.

11 NOVEMBER 1706.

Today, I have removed my family from the clutches of
Mrs. Grant to a far, far safer place. I will explain.

Some eight years ago, in 1698, Mr. William Speirs,
merchant of Dundee was persuaded by the honeyed words
of certain town-fathers and the printed broad-sheets dis-
tributed by gentlemen from Edinburgh, to sink his entire

There was an Iron Rod made about the bigness of one for a Bed,
as long as the Elephant, from the Forehead to the Point of the Tail,
being 14 Foot, which pass'd in at the fore-part of the Scull above
the Hole for the Root of the Trunk, and run back amidst the fore
Cellules, passing along the lower part of the Seat of the Brain, and
going out at the lower part of the Hole for the Spinal Marrow."

Sirs, should you require to mount an Elephant, you will learn
all that is needed in Dr. Blair's Essay; you should just know that
there were several such rods of iron inserted at convenient places
in the Elephant's body; there were wires which held the heavier
bones – including a most ingenious device which permitted the
lower jaw-bone to be raised and lowered as if the dead animal was
enjoying some ghostly meal. We are ancient now, but we remember
in our youth the wonder of these contrivances, and the semblance
of life in the skeleton. Dr. Blair mounted 260 bones, weighing in
total 312 pounds 13 ounces and 7 draps. He proceeded methodically
to connect the head, the lower jaw, the upper part of the skull, the
vertebrae and ribs and so on, using leather-straps, iron rods and
wires:

"In joining the Bones of the Foot, I took special care to hide the
Wires, so that none might appear to the Beholders," writes our pre-
eminent Surgeon.

Such close attention to detail, Mr. Orum – that was the thing!
Iron and leather, not sawdust and wool.

capital in the fund to establish a colony at Darien in the West Indies. Mr. Speirs was not alone in this – many men from these parts invested money with the 'Company of Scotland Trading to Africa and the Indies', since the scheme seemed sound. You will be appreciative, doubt-less, of the degree of success which was met there. It is Miss Gloag's unsympathetic opinion that those who had promoted and subscribed to the scheme had "been born with their heids up their *****"; I cannot express my-self so coarsely; but it seems to me that a man had best be cautious when approached by gentlemen promising untold riches. As it was, I had no capital to contribute to the Company – neither in 1698, nor now – and so I did not suffer a loss so great as some whose name in Dundee is now merely dust. Even those who did not lose all, lost much – among them being Alexander Blair and George Yeaman; and Mr. William Speirs, the father of Miss Samuella Speirs. Dr. Blair, who may have had the money, but had more sense, and frequently expresses his opinion that every one of the one-and-thirty Commissioners who treated for the Union of the Kingdoms, had lost their money in New Caledonia, and now grasp this opportu-nity, offered them by the English Queen, to salvage their fortunes.[93]

---

93. We tire, Mr. Orum, we tire of your relentless disparagement of the Gentlemen of Scotland. Certainly, the Darien Scheme was a brave but foolish enterprise that should never have been contemplated by men of sound business sense. Notwithstanding which, the very suggestion that the far-sighted gentlemen who negotiated the Act of Union might have had their own profit in mind, is, once again, libellous, monstrous and odious. Your cock-eyed wisdom has nothing to do with the dissection and study of the

All this being so, in 1700, when the magnitude of the catastrophe had become apparent, Mr. Speirs was obliged to move his family from a splendid town-house to a small set of rooms in a tenement up Tannery Close; Mrs. Speirs has ever since lamented her family's fate to all who would listen, and poor Miss Samuella was greatly mortified. I had disappointed her by marrying Hellen, seven years earlier; and her father's tumble did nothing to advance her prospects of marriage to any other.

In the Spring months of this present year, Mr. William Speirs set off for Glasgow, to manage some affairs. His wife and family were confident that such business as he conducted there would restore their fortunes; open the doors and hearts of the eligible bachelors of the valley of the Clyde; and launch young Master James Speirs into the honourable profession of tobacco-merchant. It was in full expectation, then, of a providential turn, that Mrs. Speirs received a letter from Mr. Speirs, in the first days of November, delivered by a youth who had just met the coach from Glasgow. The letter in question was confident-ly opened at the door, as Mrs. Speirs surrounded herself with her neighbours, to whom she was about to announce the family's imminent departure for the West; but, after several moments, there was a shriek loud enough to set the seagulls flying from every roof-top around and have them wheel in a cloud over the river for a full hour; for the letter brought startling news.

It seemed that Mr. Speirs had failed in his attempts to

Elephant of Dundee. Keep, Mr. Orum, to that which you know something of – if indeed, there is anything you know something of? – and leave the management of Scotland to your betters.

revive his fortunes; had failed so dramatically, indeed, that
he had been obliged to take ship to America, to escape
certain creditors. The ship had sailed on the last day of
October, and the letter had been dated on that very day;
Mr. Speirs further noted to his wife that he had encountered a fellow-passenger for the Colonies, a young widow
named Mrs. Fennell "who has a robust constitution and
is not without charm"; he hoped she would succour him
"as a companion only, in the months of hardship ahead".
(Such details as these were soon broadcast in every close,
and up and down every stair in Dundee, as the farewell
note which dropped from Mrs. Speirs's lifeless fingers
was eagerly scanned by her neighbours, at least one of
whom could do her letters).

In one moment, the dreams of Mrs. Speirs and her
children were dashed, as a man's brains are dashed out
when he falls below the hooves of a runaway horse.

In adversity, Charity and Sense frequently lose their
way. Within a day or two of the unhappy letter arriving, the Speirs family was in motion. Samuella made up
her mind that she would marry the Kirkgate piper, Mr.
Potter: Miss Speirs has determined to share with him the
sounds of his laments and to admire the contents of his
voluminous – but rarely open – purse. We all hope both
partners will have satisfaction at last. To that end, the
first Banns were read out two weeks ago – the marriage
takes place shortly.

Upon hearing of her daughter's proposal, Mrs.
Speirs sought out Mrs. Grant – the two women are old
acquaintances; a convenient arrangement was made between them. This arrangement was that Gilbert Orum
and his family would be evicted, and Mrs. Speirs and

her cadaverous son George would take possession of our room. It was all decided without reference to myself. I returned one evening to find that notice had been served for the end of the quarter; I was relieved, but dared not show it. My own arrangement with Mrs. Grant was fast unravelling my mind. But I had no answer to my wife's hopeless question: "But what shall we do now, Gilbert? We have no home."

It was my brother Hendrie who suggested the solu-tion, last week as the rain poured down outside and the rival companies of Elephant-makers sat snugly within the Hall of Rarities. "Gibby," said he, "this would make a grand home, ken?" He indicated the Hall itself. It was dry, warm, quiet, spacious. I argued with him quietly, lest we be overheard by Menteith, who was eyeing us in a superior fashion from his jumble of bones. I pointed out that the Hall belonged to Mr. Duncan, turnip-magnate. "Does it though?" asked my brother slyly. He set forth his logic, which would have done credit to Mr. Dundas, Writer to the Signet in the Kirk-gate: the turnip-store may have belonged to Mr. Duncan, he said, but it had been made over to the town for to be the Hall of Rarities; and then the town had handed over possession to Dr. Blair, for to mount the Elephant and display the bones of all worthies, in perpetuity. "It disnae belong tae naebody, ken?"

At that crowning moment of his argument, one of his children burst in, announcing breathlessly that its mother required Hendrie's immediate attendance – or, said the child, "she'll hae ye stuffed an a', she says." I was left alone to ponder the legal position. If we moved in to a quiet corner of the Hall, Mr. Duncan could not object, for the

Hall was not his; Mr. Yeaman could not object, for the Hall was not his; Dr. Blair could not object, for the Hall was not his; neither could Dr. Blair and Mr. Yeaman ever agree to evict us, for that would imply agreement between them on a matter related to the Elephant.

Today, therefore, we have moved into our new home. We have constructed two small rooms in the corner behind our slowly-rising Last Elephant, using old turnip-sacks, boxes and other items which came to hand. The sacks of wool form our beds. It is peaceful here, there are no draughts. My family and I will speedily recover from our recent ordeal – I refer not to the fire, which was bad enough; but to the several days of residence with my brother's family; and the several weeks in the bakery.

I DECEMBER 1706.

The Last Elephant lives again. She stands, in every limb, curve, shadow and wrinkle, as she did before.

Over the past four months the brothers Orum, and Mr. Fairweather, have laboured hard. Never since his earliest days have I seen Hendrie work with such enthusiasm. Even his wife Margaret was impressed. For my part, I have encouraged and criticized, cajoled and improved; head and *Proboscis* were formed, then each leg, and finally the main mass of the body; then stitching was done; until at last a resembling Elephant began to arise. Last week, two coloured pieces of glass were inserted for the Elephant's eyes, especially commissioned from a craftsman out the Forfar road – "no expense shall be spared!" exclaimed Mr. Yeaman with great vehemence. The skin of the left fore-foot, after its many adventures, had fallen apart as soon as we touched it. We were therefore obliged to fit a wooden-leg, acquired from Mr. Ogilvie, the ships' chandler; the wooden leg is finely crafted and greatly admired, especially by sailors. Eyes inserted and twinkling in the winter sunshine, wooden leg firmly on the floor – it was almost as if the tragic beast had been led in from the street by Mr. Santos and Giovanni, for to perform her tricks. Watty Fairweather wept with joy, then disappeared for two days to drink away his sorrows.

The impecunious of Dundee have brought their Elephant to life; but Dr. Blair and Menteith still struggle with their skeleton. As I write these words, comfortable within our new home, I observe that they have still considerable work to do. With some feeling of pleasure

do I await Dr. Blair's call to draw and engrave their skeleton, for there is no one else with my skills in all of Forfar-
shire; the surgeon is greatly displeased, I expect, by this
notion.[94]

I have only one concern on this best of days: in the
construction of all of Dr. Blair's iron frame-work, Mr.
Lockhart the black-smith has played the major part. Mr.
Lockhart came frequently to the 'Hall of Rarities' to consult with Dr. Blair; on those occasions when I was also
there, Mr. Lockhart would look at me with a meaningful
stare, and nod heavily at the gradually diminishing pile of
loose bones on one hand, and the slowly increasing shape
of the mounted skeleton on the other hand. I did my best
to appear a party to his conspiracy; and then bent my head
to my work on the pelt. Dr. Blair once told us that an
Elephant is renowned for its long memory of promises
and of injuries; Mr. Lockhart clearly demonstrates a similar nature.

---

94. We are enraged, but not astonished, at Mr. Orum's mendacious
pretensions. 'The impecunious of Dundee', indeed! Who, other than
our own Dr. Blair and Mr. Yeaman, had the *Foresight* to preserve
the Elephant? Who, other than our own merchants and lawyers,
and many respected citizens, provided the *Capital* with which to
set up the skeleton, the skin and the Hall of Rarities? We find it
unlikely that Dr. Blair, a man of Learning, Philosophy and Christian
Charity, would have had any feelings of 'displeasure' at the thought
of employing an engraver whose drafts, in the words of our Surgeon,
were "coarse" and whose plates "might have been done finer in
London". Let it not be forgotten that Dr. Blair, in his Essay, has
acknowledged the work of Mr. Orum and of those who stuffed the
skin; he at least recognizes the debt – Mr. Orum, it seems does not.

7 DECEMBER 1706.

It is my birthday today, and I sit in the Hall of Rarities, contemplating – as I always do on this day in the year – the Passage of Time. I sit in the darkness. We now take the greatest care with candles and fires, and my daughter Agnes takes it upon herself to go round the Hall whenever we enter or leave it, and especially in preparation for sleep, in search of the slightest stray spark which might kindle – once again – the bonfire of our calamities.

A few minutes ago, the Last Elephant awoke.

"Gilbert," she said, placing her trunk gently upon my shoulder, "you did not fail me. I AM the Ultimate Elephant, the chief of the ways of God, and you have saved me from the Emptiness."

I inclined my head, feeling humbly that I had done all that a man could do: this year of my life has not been wasted.

"But what," she continued, "is that thing that stands down there?" She lifted her wooden left fore-foot and waved it heavily in the direction of the skeleton of Dr. Blair.

I explained that those were her own bones, mounted for Philosophical Experiment by Dr. Blair. In response, the Last Elephant lifted her feet and limped noisily down the Hall. The earth shook with her movement. As she came beside the bones, she stopped, raised her trunk and tapped the right *Scapula*. I was, I admit, astonished. With great stiffness of movement, the Skeleton stirred.

"Ah," it croaked, with some haughtiness. "The Pelt."

"Ah," replied the Last Elephant, "the Bones."

The two relics of the Elephant slowly circled each other, much as two dogs or cats might do, in preparation for friendship or a fight. My mother, who now sleeps in the greatest luxury in a room of her own, called out to ask me what the beasts were up to. I had no answer. We watched together in silence.

"A rash undertaking," said my Elephant, prodding here and there among the bones with her *Proboscis.*

"Coarse, very coarse," wheezed Dr. Blair's Elephant, elevating and lowering her jaw by means of its cunning wires.

"The Royal Society in London," declared my Elephant, "will find much philosophical amusement at your appearance."

The Bones made no response at first, but then observed with a laugh that rattled and echoed through the Hall, that "Alas, madam, our engraver will have much work to do to make your portrait acceptable to those learned gentlemen."

"Madam," replied my Elephant, "your mounting is but a weak endeavour."

"We might say of you," stated the skeleton, "that the undertaking has been bold, but the performance mean."[95]

---

95. We have observed once before that certain words and phrases from Dr. Blair's momentous Essay have somehow found their way into Orum's devilish narrative: we cannot speculate how this came about. But consider Dr. Blair's closing address to Sir Hans Sloane:

"And thus, Sir, I have finish'd these my Weak Endeavours: The Undertaking, I doubt, will seem bold to some, and rash to others, and the Performance mean. But the many Obligations you have laid upon me, and the frequent Marks of Esteem I have received in your

"But you can barely move," rumbled my Elephant. "Your bones are locked in iron, you are bound as in a cage."

The Skeleton looked at the Pelt. "As for you," it muttered, "your skin fits ill, you have a wooden leg, and you seem to have lost much of your shape." This was true, I fear: the Pelt had been tanned with little care, and had shrunk while in the possession of Mr. Yeaman; and despite the best efforts of Watty is still tight in places. In order to preserve the beauty of the living creature in my engravings, I will be obliged to make some alterations to my drawings.

My Elephant made no further utterance, but continued slowly to nudge at each bone with her trunk, much to the annoyance of the Skeleton, which rattled threateningly at each unwelcome touch. At length my mother, raising herself from her bed and walking with great difficulty the length of the Hall, led my Elephant back to its position, talking quietly to her as she did so. The Skeleton, casting from its empty eye-sockets one last glance in our direction, clattered its toes, then resumed its stance.

———•———

several Letters, made me pass over all Obstacles, Reflections, and Discouragements, when to serve you and your honourable Society was my only Design. I have rather chosen to address you in a plain and common Stile, than give the least suspicion of Disingenuity in a finer Language; especially since it is History I have written, where Matter of Fact, and not Romance, where Eloquence, is the chief Design."

Contrast, if you will, Sirs, Dr. Blair's humility and eloquence, with what you have just read. So much for Romance!

We find Mr. Orum's Journal far-fetched and wearisome, and we will not indulge him by printing any more of the journal for this date, in which he leads us only into the Labyrinth of Insanity. He has insulted us with Phantasms. He has peddled Gossip and Scandal about people in whom we have no interest at all; and fed us Libel and Lies about people to whom Great Britain owes its supremacy. Since the man struck out on his own, and deluded himself with a sense of importance that was no more than a shine, a gloss upon his character, he has boasted of this and boasted of that. In his next entry he will swell himself again with the inflated sense of worth that is the mark of every man who has lost humility. We have not lost humility, we are proud to say: in that respect we are far better than most.

16 JANUARY 1707.[96]

My work upon the engraving of the skeleton was delayed while we worked on the pelt; but I found the hours of the evening sufficient for that; and today, on the sixteenth day of January in the year 1707, on a bitter day on which our breath froze in our throats; the Hall of Rarities has been opened up for all those who would wish to come and admire the Elephant. Dr. Blair, having scoffed at our work these past few months, was obliged to show some respect for our endeavours. On seeing the two ghosts of the Elephant side by side in the Hall, he today regretted aloud that it had not been possible to fit the skin over the skeleton like a coat, to be buttoned up and buttoned down at pleasure; for such an interesting exhibit would, he did not doubt, give rise to a whole new generation of philosophers, who would accordingly be inspired to go and unbutton all the other coated mysteries of the Earth. For my part, I shudder even to think of what inquiring devils we might raise, whose only concern was flaying the skin off living creatures, in order to be enlightened on what went on underneath: for once the skin is off, there is no return or repair. Where will all this Enlightenment

---

96. On this day in 1707, in Edinburgh and London, our patriotic Parliaments voted in favour of the Act of Union. And in Dundee, the 'Hall of Rarities' was thrown open to the crowds of eager citizens. We should consign Mr. Orum's further remarks on this day to the 'Footnotes', for, in the Grand Sweep of *History*, they are worth no more than that. However, pursuant to our Editorial Duty, we must – against all Reason – exercise *Charity*.

end and all this Philosophy, I wonder, if we send out our
children to lay bare every last bone upon the land and
under the sea: would there be any creature remaining to
crawl, to pounce, to swim, to fly? Would there remain any
single animal or beast to pace the wilds in majesty, any
bird to soar in the heavens and sing, any fish to dart and
glide and bubble? Or would all the Beasts of the Earth
end up in the Hall of Rarities, no more among the quick,
always among the dead?

26 JANUARY 1707.

In that first week of display, all of Dundee – and half of Broughty Ferry – came through the door of the Hall of Rarities; to admire and depart astounded; but not astounded enough, I found, since not one of them fully understood the craftsmanship, the ingenuity, and the labour, which this representation had cost us all. It was, however, of some pleasure to me, to be able to display some of my drawings of the Elephant, both of the individual bones, and of the Elephant as it now stood in doubled display. These drawings met with universal approval; and many a man came and shook my hand, a tear in his eyes occasioned by the beauty of my representations and their great likeness to the living creature; I was able to sell some of these works to the better class of people.[97]

Mr. Yeaman attended in state, bringing with him all the fawning Councillors of his party.[98] I believe that his original intent and purpose was to have the pelt cut into smaller parts, and made up into horsewhips as presents for such friends as would speed his way to Parliament. But that may not be true: others have voiced the opinion that Mr. Yeaman had hoped to have the seats and panels of his carriage covered with the leather, as if he were

---

97. And now we have it, Mr. Orum! For all your concerns about the Last Elephant, and the methods of Dr. Blair, all that now satisfies you is money! – a profit which you have made only because Dr. Blair had the foresight and the energy to undertake his astonishing task.

98. If a man is not at liberty to fawn in the company of a great Politician, what hope then for Society?

thereby travelling within the Elephant; still others that the skin of *Florentia* was intended to grace the feet of his wife. Whatever private resolution he had made on that day last April had been conquered by his desire to appear as the most public-spirited man in all of Forfar-shire.[99]

---

99. Dr. Blair, by contrast, was pleased to report in his Essay that:

"The chief endeavour of Provost Yeaman was to preserve the Skin whole, in order to Stuff it (which is now done to so good purpose and so lively, that it is become a most curious Ornament, as the Figure after the Original, which now stands in our Hall, doth represent)."

Whom, we wonder, should we believe – Mr. Orum, with his mean-spirited repetition of idle and envious gossip; or Dr. Blair with his keen and generous insight into the mind of a man who was then Provost and who rose to become our Parliamentary Member in Westminster?

2 MARCH 1707.

One week after the opening of the Hall of Rarities, the number of visitors had rapidly diminished. I know this for a certainty, since Mr. Yeaman – contrary to the express wish of Dr. Blair – offered me a position as Custodian to the Hall: to open it up at two o'clock on a Wednesday afternoon and Saturday afternoon; to charge a fee for entrance of one penny Scots; to maintain vigilance that no one clambered upon the stuffed exhibit, or touched the bones, or made off with any of them – "we would not like to lose that fore-foot again, Mr. Orum!" he laughed, much to my shame; to raise and lower such parts of the Elephant's anatomy as had been left mobile by Dr. Blair's contrivances; and to lock the door firmly at six o'clock. There was to be no payment for this service, but the arrangement was greatly convenient, for it legally confirmed our domestic situation.

Which situation is comfortable, since Hendrie has (I asked not how) come by some long lengths of dyed cloth, which he has hung from the roof as walls for our rooms. I have created a third room, in which my family spend their days, leaving us with two bedrooms. We have furniture created from boxes and seats stuffed with wool. Hellen is contented: we have never lived in more than one room before now. The only difficulty we have is that the two Elephants engage nightly in sonorous argument, which frightens the children very much. Rarely, however, do the Elephants approach each other: they call out insults and epithets from one end of the Hall to the other. My mother frequently intercedes. I comfort my children by reminding them that the ghostly sounds at night keep at bay any passing scoundrels, robbers or murderers.

In the first week, when we opened the Hall every afternoon, my takings amounted to two Pounds seventeen Shillings and seven-pence Scots. In the second week, I took but eighteen Shillings and six-pence (and three clipped coins of Irish provenance). In the third, when we opened the Hall only on two afternoons, the purse totalled one bawbee, or six-pence. At that time, Mr. Yeaman decided that there should be no set hours of opening, but that I would, if required, admit the casual visitor and relieve him of his money, which would duly be handed over to the Town-Council.[100]

---

100. We have uncovered a remarkable instance of one such 'casual visitor' in the archives of the town-house. In November of 1715, while the Earl of Mar marched around the Northern Counties of Scotland raising *Rebellion*, the stuffed Elephant in the Hall of Rarities met its end. On a stormy afternoon, a visitor paid his fee and entered the Hall of Rarities; the rising wind caught the open door and wrenched it from the hand of Mr. Steuart, who was at that time Town-Clerk and Custodian of the Rarities; the tumultuous wind struck the Elephant, and toppled it to the ground with such violence that it burst apart, hurling straw and wool into the face of the visitor, and the pieces of skin to the four corners of the Hall. The newcomer was observed to turn deathly pale; to utter a curse in the French language; and then flee the scene of desolation. Mr. Steuart contended that the visitor was none other than 'Old Pretender', Prince James, who perhaps saw in the Explosion an omen of his failing invasion. Mr. Steuart was resolutely persuaded that, from that day onwards, no foreigner should ever again be permitted to enter the Hall of Rarities – a most sensible instance of a *Bye-Law*, which our present City Fathers would be wise to take notice of. However, let us not omit to observe that Mr. Orum's

I MAY 1707.

Today, the first day of May 1707, Queen Anne in London is pleased to unite her Scottish and English Kingdoms, and meet with a united Parliament in London. To celebrate this day, which has in truth met rather with ill-concealed anger than public demonstrations of joy, our Provost Mr. Yeaman proposed a short party of reconciliation between himself, Mr. Alexander Blair and Dr. Patrick Blair, and a small number of Mr. Yeaman's most dedicated support- ers. To my very great surprise, I received an invitation to attend this celebration; almost was my dear Hellen car- ried away forever at this honour!

It became clear this morning that my attendance was as licensed recorder of the day's happy events, as I was en- joined to bring along the tools of my trade and "make free with them". The day could not have dawned in brighter aspect: "such an auspicious day for the future of a great United Kingdom!" exclaimed Mr. Yeaman, to his assem- bled guests. From adherents of the 'Country Party' and the dispossessed King, there were jeers of opprobrium; from the 'Unionists' there were loud cheers of approba- tion; by those who cared neither one way nor another, but who had high hopes of the food and drink awaiting them, hats and sticks were thrown in the air – "Long Live Great-Britain!" was the cry of the day.

---

proud memorial barely lasted longer than nine years: the pelt, now unstuffed, was consigned to a dusty corner of the Hall. The skeleton, we need scarcely add, remained fixed to the floor, and shivered not an inch. So much for Craftsmanship

Mr. Yeaman assembled us in 'his' Hall of Rarities where, surrounded by clouds of dust, and before the stuffed pelt of the Elephant, he read out to us each and every one of the five-and-twenty Articles of the Act of Union. This took some time. Mr. Yeaman lingered long and lovingly over any mention of 'the Parliament of Great-Britain'; made much of the promised "full freedom of trade and navigation, to and from any port or place within the said United Kingdom, and the dominions and plantations thereunto belonging"; and drew gasps of astonishment at the liberality of the Queen, in paying to Scotland the sum of £398,085 10s as an 'equivalent' – some said it was to pay for excise on liquor, others said it was to buy the Commissioners. There were grumblings when certain measures anent ale, salt, malt and coal were announced; and many shook their heads, judging that "it will never last", at the news that there would henceforward be common coin, weights and measures. Some stupefac-tion met the Article in which the sum of £1,997,763 8s 4½d (Sterling) was mentioned as being the amount in tax which Parliament had to raise in England; and all felt that Scotland had done well to escape from that tax to the tune only of £48,000.

———•———

For once, and once only, Mr. Orum's remarks accurately record the main and material points of an event in the his-tory of our Great Kingdom. What remains of Mr. Orum's Journal for this day is, put simply, of no value. As a vignette of the mood of the Nation on that glorious day, it is of little concern to Friends of History. Those Gentlemen who, finding themselves with time to spare – and we must ask seriously why they find themselves idle? – may continue their reading in the footnotes. There is only one matter in Mr. Orum's scribbled concoction which requires our attention. This concerns 'Mr. Green, the English Pirate', to whom Dr. Blair refers in a moment of 'gallows' humour: we suppose that the ever-present danger of being afloat disturbed the surgeon's harmonious equilibrium.[101] The man Green to whom Dr. Blair refers is Thomas Green, who suffered the mis-fortune of being captured, tried and hanged as a pirate in 1705, at a time of high passion in Leith. Such unfortunate mis-understandings no longer occur, now that Britannia Rules the Waves, although we understand that Leith is still a place to be avoided.[102]

---

101. We have elsewhere noted the dangers of ill-considered voyages upon the sea. We base our warnings upon mis-adventures such as the one Mr. Orum describes. In recent times, we will recall the fate of two dozen young ladies of Inverness, who in 1802 set sail on a Saturday to visit their swains in Beauly: we understand that they were never seen again. We refer you, should our word be doubted, to a sorrowful lament of that year, which tells us how

> *'Four-and-twenty virgins set out from Inverness [...]*
> *When the night was over, there were four-and-twenty less.'*

102. Mr. Orum writes: "When all Articles had been read out to the fractious crowd, the party moved in procession, under a pale blue sky and a bright sun, to the harbour; where several tables were set up on the wharf, covered with all the best that Mr. Yeaman could pillage from the resources of the Town-hall. For what particular reason I could never establish, Mr. Yeaman had also laid on 'short pleasure-trips upon the Tay' for his invited guests. To this end, a boat had been freshly-painted and decorated in the colours of the Union, and a strange new ensign fluttered from its mast. The boat was but a small one, and could hold perhaps five or six people at a time. To inaugurate this entertainment, Mr. Yeaman selected

three of the most honoured guests: Mr. Alexander Blair, Dr. Patrick Blair and Mr. James Robertson; and then crooked a finger at me, indicating that I was to accompany them and immortalize the events of this most glorious of days. My children, who had been forced to join in the merriment, cried bitter tears in fearful anticipation that their father would never return from this voyage.

"As we stepped aboard, all except Mr. Yeaman were greatly discomfited to find that the captain of this craft – he who was to manoeuvre the boat upon the face of the waters – was none other than Hendrie Orum, my brother. To my certain knowledge, Hendrie had never spent any time at sea, apart from a fishing voyage to Crail in the summer of 1700, from which he returned shaking – a brush with death to which his wife attributed the birth of their son David, in the following year.

"However, no protest was made; Mr. Yeaman confidently announced that Hendrie was a faithful and skilled lieutenant 'who had proved himself'; the day seemed set fair; and Hendrie untied from the shore in quite naval manner. To the great cheers of those pleased enough now to be left ashore, we quitted the harbour of Dundee and ventured forth upon the calm waters of the Tay. A cool breeze sprang up as we came out, and soon we were bowling in lively fashion back and forth between Fife-shire and Forfar-shire. Mr. Yeaman had not omitted to bring along a basket full of the best foods and wines; and soon he and his principal guests were sitting back and reflecting in good humour upon the state of Britain.

"There was some discussion on whether the new Union would prove for Scotland a good thing, or a bad. Opinions being fairly divided between Mr. Yeaman and Mr. Blair; and Dr. Blair now cautiously attacking both positions; Mr. Robertson chose to state that all men were sinners, and that it mattered little whether there be a Union. It was Mr. Yeaman's strong opinion that a Scotchman in the new 'Great-Britain' would have to put himself out, to prove that he was as good as the Englishman; Dr. Blair argued that the duty of a Scotchman would be to prove himself better than the Englishman; Mr. Blair declared that a Scotchman need do neither; Mr. Robertson re-iterated his position on Man and Sin. The discussion was lively; but, as our captain sailed us up and down, not one of the party was willing to strike out for victory in the debate. For my part, I was permitted a mug of ale and a leg of chicken, but was careful not to let the grease from the latter affect my graphical duties. Hendrie made free with several mugs of ale, a bottle of dark rum, and – as an after-thought – some slices of bread and beef; to such an extent did he enjoy himself that we soon found ourselves stuck upon a sand-bank at a distance half-way between Dundee and Wormit.

"Hendrie expressed great surprise at this mis-adventure, but was optimistic that the tide would soon float us off; his passengers settled down to a pleasant fore-noon on a gentle sea under a warm sun.

"As the hours went by, it became clear that the tide would not in fact release us; and that we were caught fast. Mr. Alexander Blair took the sun and complained loudly of the burning of his face; Mr. Robertson sat in silence and read in the Bible which he had brought with him; Dr. Blair covered himself with a napkin and advised his ship-mates to do the same; Mr. Yeaman launched a lengthy tirade against the services rendered, past and present, by Hendrie; who said nothing at all, but gazed distractedly over the waters of the Tay, to all appearance remembering voyages to distant ports and spice-islands (the isle of Mugdrum being the most exotic of these). And then, almost without warning, a sea-mist, or haar, came at us from the east, a fast, curling, freezing, damp cloud that enveloped us from one moment to the next. Hendrie, Mr. Yeaman and Mr. Blair threw themselves into a panic, while Dr. Blair tried to re-assure them that, while we were still stuck fast on the sand-bank, no harm could come to us; indeed, Hendrie regained sufficient confidence to argue that his lack of seaman-ship had in fact been their salvation; Mr. Yeaman had by then lost sufficient philosophy that he was inclined to agree with him.

"More hours went by. Mr. Robertson read aloud all the verses in the Book of Jonah. Dr. Blair kept our spirits high by wondering whether, were we to free ourselves and land upon the shore of Dundee from the mist, we might suffer the same fate, on this historic day, as that of the unfortunate Mr. Green, the English pirate: 'The people of Dundee, Mr. Yeaman, are not so easily pleased by this Act of Union,' he cautioned, 'And may even now be searching for those who have robbed Scotland of all pride'. At which thought, both Mr. Yeaman and Mr. Alexander Blair – so far as he was able under his burned skin – turned pale. 'You do not think, Patrick – ?' muttered Mr. Yeaman – but was unable to give voice to his oppressive thoughts. Dr. Blair merely shrugged in a gesture of fatalism: 'If the people believe that Scotland is alive with such spying wretches as that Mr. Defoe, vile monster and prostituted wretch of London, then they will stop at nothing to root them out.' Mr. Alexander Blair submitted that it might be safer to land upon the Fife shore? Dr. Blair thought that there would be no great advantage to that: 'the feeling of Scotland is much the same on either side of the Tay, I fear.' Mr. Robertson gave no comfort to anyone by reminding us of the fate of sinful Archbishop Sharp, executed by saints near St. Andrews: 'Not far from here, gentlemen.'

"More hours went by; and then from the mist came a snorting sound, then a shout; Hendrie shouted back, greatly relieved. After several more minutes of like shouting; in which confusing sailor's terms were used by our unseen rescuer, and little understood by my brother; a boat appeared quite close to us, from out of the haar. The captain of this vessel was none other than Mr. Campbell, the fish-merchant; it seemed he had been dispatched to look for us by certain concerned residents of Dundee, who, establishing that all of the food and drink had vanished down their throats without their Joy at the Union being in any way diminished, now looked to their host for replenishment; and found him missing. Taking a bearing upon the spot where we had last been seen, Mr. Campbell had sailed out and, after several false casts, had come upon us. It was a matter now of throwing us a stout rope, which Hendrie, seeing a chance to redeem himself in the eyes of his patron, made fast in skilled manner; and then, with the application of oars and sails, we were pulled off and taken back to the harbour of Dundee; to be welcomed; not as pirates, but as heroes; by a crowd anxious for more refreshment on this first day of the prosperous United Kingdom. Mr. Robertson stepped from the boat and kissed the bare earth in great solemnity; Mr. Yeaman, thankful to have lived to see the evening of the great day, was not slow to order up additional fuel for celebration; Hendrie was welcomed ashore as the man of the hour; Mr. Campbell even more so; and the carousing continued.

"In the excitement of our trial upon the sea, I regret to say that I threw over-board such drawings and notes as I had made of the foremost persons and scenes of the day, in a vain attempt to lift the boat from the sand-bank. But no one concerned themselves with this loss, until Mr. Campbell, in genial mood at his popular success, joked aloud that I had lost these drawings in much the same way as I had lost the left fore-foot of the Elephant. After making this public announcement, he inhaled snotter with great liveliness, and beamed upon me. Dr. Patrick Blair looked at me inhospitably, then took Mr. Campbell to one side to ask him a few questions."

31 DECEMBER 1707.

We have at last, Sirs, reached the end of Mr. Orum's ram-
bling and self-aggrandizing Journal, insofar as it concerns
the Elephant of Dundee and the Affairs of 1707. We will
not do Mr. Orum the honour of printing the remaining
dross of his journal, for the matters contained therein are
of little interest to us: in any case, those papers are now
lost. Orum has brought us to the end of a glorious year in
the History of Great Britain – although the casual reader
of Orum's works would scarcely appreciate that Great
Deeds had taken place. We have suffered so far with this
narration, dear Friends of History, and we hope that 'By
its Darkness, we have seen Light'. It has been our Duty as
Editor, and certainly not our Pleasure, to have presented
Mr. Orum's troubled thoughts to the world: with a heavy
heart and a sense of unqualified relief, we do so one last
time. In this one last, scurrilous, infantile and confusing entry, Orum constructs another fable to mis-lead us.
Once you have read it, consider this: our family has had
in its possession for more than a century a splendid walk-
ing-stick of which the iron blade is formed in elephantine
manner; would our own ancestor have been taken in so
easily by the man who sold it to them, as Orum suggests
below? We think not. So much for Deception.[103]

---

103. Mr. Orum concludes: "It is the last night of the year of 1707.
My work to preserve the Last Elephant is complete. I am as poor
now as I was when first I set pen to these pages. My drawings are
done, my engravings have been taken by Dr. Blair for his own profit.
In the 'Hall of Rarities', for all time, stands the embodiment of
Florentia.

"But before I close the year, I must reveal one thing more: this concerns my debt to the black-smith, Mr. Lockhart. Mr. Lockhart had placed me in a position where I felt obliged to acquire for him some distinctive bones of the Elephant; from which he might make moulds; and thus a fortune for himself in selling castings of parts of the skeleton to the better houses of Dundee. I had, of course, no opportunity to provide him with what he wanted; the only osseous item which ever came my way was the left fore-foot, which was safely returned to the custody of, and for annotation by, Dr. Blair. Mr. Lockhart had been intimately involved in the matters relating to the mounting of the skeleton, and had seen the animal rise again from the pile of bones in the corner of the Hall; he knew, therefore, that no leg was missing, no jaw-bone, no tail, not one toe. On several days, he looked at me significantly, and I feared that I would not longer be able to practise my trade as engraver here in Dundee: for he is a man of large frame. It was only when left alone in the Hall of Rarities in our new domestic arrangement that I hit upon an agreeable solution.

"In a dark corner of the Hall, Dr. Blair had caused to have stored, in wooden chests, his collection of the bones of other dead animals and small children. I believe that his good wife had finally demanded that they be removed from the house, now that the family was growing in size, and the boy had reached impressionable age. Accordingly, two dozen or more boxes had been carted up from the house, just as soon as we came into possession of the Hall; these boxes form a solid wall for our rooms; each had been carefully labelled – in Latin words, so that the ordinary citizen should not be alarmed – with a brief description of its osteological contents: '*Equus admissarius*', '*Bos non intacta (Forfariensis)*', '*Puella intra octo annos*', '*Ovicula robusta (Balmeriniensis)*', '*Puer duodecem annos excessit (Lunaniensis)*' and so forth. In twilight moments, furnished with a candle, I examined the contents of the boxes; but of most interest to me was one which was labelled '*Miscellanea MDCCIII*', and which contained a number of bones clearly from several skeletons. It was an easy task to remove one of these bones; it was possibly the

Humerus of a donkey; it would not be missed; and in a matter of an hour or so, to use a sharpened knife and my engraver's tools to carve it into the realistic shape of a bone which – indeed – had always been missing from *Florentia*.

"Mr. Lockhart did not know; for few, other than Mr. Sutherland, had ever asked; whether our Elephant had been male or female; nor did anyone know, who had not been acquainted with Dr. Moulins's published work on his Irish Elephant, whether the male Elephant ever possessed such an astonishingly large bone as I now produced from the osteological collection. Mr. Lockhart was greatly impressed; to his credit, he blushed on seeing it; but soon overcame his natural modesty and set to the task of imitating it in brass, in copper, in iron; turning the metal likenesses into candle-sticks, bed-warmers, festive tankards, stocks for guns, ink-wells; and many other goods which his fertile imagination showed him.

"These items now grace the studies and bedrooms of gentlemen and scholars in Dundee, St. Andrews, Dysart; even, I am told, in Edinburgh and Oxford. Mr. Lockhart, like several others, will make his fortune from our Elephant in the Hall of Rarities. But not Gilbert Orum, engraver of Dundee; who now sits in the warm shadow of the Last Elephant; and rests his pen for the last time this year."

EPILOGUE:

"Postes a tergo relicti."

We omitted to mention in our letter to *The Dundee, Perth and Cupar Advertiser* the location of the 'Hall of Rarities', for fear of losing the attention of the Readers of that newspaper; through this omission, unfortunately, we cannot now remember that detail. It was not far from Dr. Blair's house, we recall, and not distant also from his famous Physic Garden, in which so many botanical specimens were cultivated – only the third such 'botanical' garden in the whole of Great Britain, succeeding upon those of Oxford and Edinburgh.

Sadly, in this present year of 1830, neither does the Hall of Rarities remain standing, nor have its contents remained undisturbed. In the year 1789 – the very year, we will recall, that *Liberty* ravished the French Nation, and all *Reason* was ultimately lost in *Regicide* – a distinguished and far-sighted agriculturist, applying the very latest science in the exercise of his profession, bid a good sum of money for all the bones contained within the Hall. Mr. Alexander Riddoch, our late Provost, was amenable to this offer; the bid was successful; the bones were removed; the Hall reverted to a store for root-vegetables; our agriculturist had all the bones ground down and scattered as a top-dressing to his fields in Strathmore. We understand that the resulting harvests were much admired. Even today, specks of the Elephant, of Provost Yeaman and of many other *Good Men*, are doubtless blowing in the autumn winds which visit Strathmore. So much for Immortality.

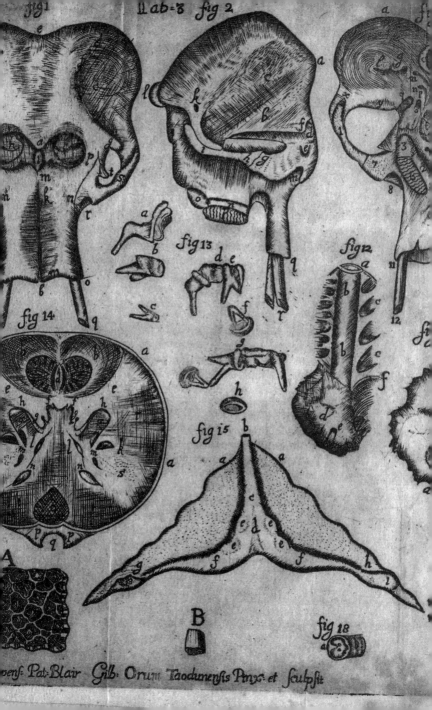

Tab: 3 fig 2

fig 13

fig 12

fig 14

fig 15

A

B

fig 18

vensf. Pat: Blair Gilb: Orum Taodunensis Pinx et sculpsit

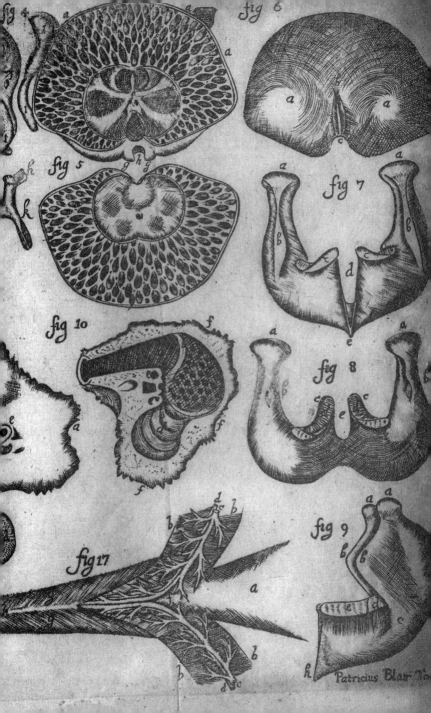

fig 4 fig 6

fig 5 fig 7

fig 10 fig 8

fig 17 fig 9

Patricius Blair Ta

HISTORICAL NOTE

Patrick Blair was born around 1675 at Lethendy, just north of Perth, Scotland. His years of study were spent in a variety of places, which included Flanders, where he was known to have worked between 1694 and 1697. He married Elizabeth Whyte in Dundee in April 1702, from which marriage a son John was born (4th June 1703). At least three further children were born – Henry, Elizabeth and Isabell. In 1712 the family moved to the small town of Coupar Angus; in the same year Patrick Blair received a doctorate from King's College Aberdeen, and was elected Fellow of the Royal Society in London.

In 1713, he travelled to London and Oxford, to meet with fellow-scientists; and in 1715 he travelled to Preston in the company of an army of Jacobites; and then to London as a prisoner-of-war. Saved from the gallows in 1716, he stayed on in London, then retired to the town of Boston in Lincolnshire, where he died in 1728.

His first major scientific publication was a very detailed account of the anatomy and 'osteology' of the elephant which died in Dundee in 1706. This account, running to well over one hundred pages, bursting with anatomical descriptions, and thick with background material on the known 'facts' about elephants, was published in two parts by the Royal Society in 1710. In later years, Patrick Blair made a number of important and respected contributions to the emerging science of Botany.

Very little is known about the life of Gilbert Orum. He was probably born around 1670. From the Parish

Registers, we have discovered the few remaining facts about him. He married Barbra Maxwell in Dundee, on 22nd July 1693. The new Mrs. Orum was the widow of Thomas Fairweather, whom she had married on 13th February 1691. Barbra must have died shortly after her wedding to Mr. Orum, since Gilbert then married Hellen Webster on 1st November 1693. From the latter marriage, five children were born: Thomas, born 26th July 1694; Agnes, born 28th March 1697; Hendrie, 17th June 1700; another Thomas – the first-born we must suppose having died – born on 10th February 1702; and finally Robert, 18th April 1708.

Gilbert had two brothers: Hendrie, who married a woman named Margaret Stratoune; and John, who was the first husband of Margaret Stratoune – they had one son, John. Hendrie and Margaret had a further eleven children: William, Alexander, Hendrie, Margaret, George, Lillias, David, Isobell, another Hendrie, Eupham, and finally another Margaret.

All that remains to us of Gilbert Orum's artistic work are the few engravings published in Dr. Blair's Essay. If you look closely at the principal engravings you will see the following words: *'Gilb. Orum Taodunensis pinxit et sculpsit'* – 'Gilbert Orum of Dundee drew and engraved this.'

ACKNOWLEDGEMENTS

I would like to thank the following people and organisa-
tions for their assistance in researching this novel:

Carol Smith, of Dundee City Libraries, for her assistance in tracking down material relating to 'Senex', the
'Hall of Rarities' and Dr. Patrick Blair;

Phil Howard, of the National Museum of Scotland in
Edinburgh, whose 30-minute crash-course in Elephant-
taxidermy was most illuminating (he is in no way to be
blamed for the crude stuffing of our Dundee Elephant);

Wendy Turner, also of the NMS in Edinburgh, whose
guided tour of the Museum's new Hall of Bubble-
Wrapped Beasts in Chambers Street suggested to me
that there is indeed an After-life;

Michael Bolik, of the University of Dundee's Archive
Services, who sought out and provided copies of the engravings of the Elephant of Dundee;

The Royal Society in London, which kindly gave
permission for the reproduction of text from their
'Philosophical Transactions' of 1710.

Those seeking further guidance on how to dissect an
Elephant, or any other mammal, or requiring more information on the life of Dr. Patrick Blair, should consult the
following works:

Mr. Patrick Blair, *Osteographia Elephantina, or a Full and
Exact Description of all the Bones of an Elephant etc.*
Published in the 'Philosophical Transactions of the
Royal Society', Volume 27. London 1710.

Patrick Blair, *Osteographia Elephantina* etc. Published
by G. Strahan, London 1713. (An off-print from the
Transactions above)

Dr. Patrick Blair, *Observations in Physic, Anatomy,
Surgery, and Botanicks*. London 1718.

Dr. Patrick Blair, *A Description of the Organ of Hearing
in the Elephant* etc. Published in the 'Philosophical
Transactions of the Royal Society', Volume 30.
London 1719.

Dr. Patrick Blair, *Botanical Essays*. London 1720.

Dr. Patrick Blair, *Pharmaco-Botanologia, an Alphabetical
and Classical Dissertation on all the British Indigenous
and Garden Plants of the New London Dispensatory*,
London 1723–1728 (in eight volumes).

Alex. P. Stevenson, *Patrick Blair – Surgeon-Apothecary,
Dundee, Scotland – A Memoir*. Dundee 1907.

ANDY DRUMMOND
Edinburgh, September 2007

First published in 2008 by Polygon,
an imprint of Birlinn Ltd
West Newington House · 10 Newington Road
Edinburgh EH9 1QS
www.birlinn.co.uk

9 8 7 6 5 4 3 2 1

The publisher acknowledges subsidy from the

 Scottish
Arts Council

towards the publication of this book.

ISBN 13: 978 1 84697 044 3

British Library Cataloguing in Publication Data
A catalogue record for this book is available on request
from the British Library.

Typeset in Custodia by Dalrymple
Printed in Sweden by Scandbook